Dummy.

©2025, Carl M. Harris

All rights reserved. This book or any portion thereof may not be reproduced or used in any manner whatsoever without the express written permission of the publisher except for the use of brief quotations in a book review.

ISBN: 979-8-35099-171-0

ISBN eBook: 979-8-35099-172-7

DUMMY.

CARL M. HARRIS

CHAPTER ONE

"So how much you tryin' to get this time?" Melvin asked, "Cause these niggas is talkin' 'bout dropping a brick off *right now* if you want it!"

"Naah yung, I ain't ready for all that right now," I replied. "I'm thinkin' the usual... quarter key yo... l ain't ready for no consignment shit right now... won't have them bammas tryin' to kill me over some 'Oh you late with my money' shit! Fuck *that*... I'll buy what I can afford to move right now... fuck the *dumb* shit."

"I don't understand you 'Los... you got what, like, four spots?? And one of 'em over East, so I *know* you gettin' money the way *them* fiends be coppin'... you need to step tha fuck up... shit, you'll get a better price *and* you won't have to keep buggin' me to re-up every three damn days!"

As much as I hated to admit it, Melvin had a point. I'd gone from grams to O's within a month mainly 'cause I didn't cook my shit to within an inch of its life...(well, that *and* because Rick hooked me up, but more on that later)... I always thought if my quality was better than the rest, I could shortstop the fiends and *still* make dough... and I did. Now, within four months, I was movin' close to a couple bricks a month without tryin' hard... other cats moved more, but they had overhead that I didn't... l sold all my shit all by myself, so I ended up makin' more even though I sold less... *and* I stayed under the radar.

While dudes were buyin' 300ZX's, Benzes, and Acuras, I was steady lookin' for an old school to push... muhfuckahs called 'em hoopties, but *I* called 'em classics, and one-time didn't give me a second look, even though I had more money tied up in 'em then that brand new '93 whatever' that Tommy Lumplump just bought... plus, me bein' from Cleveland *and* hangin' in DC so much had me stuck on old schools... I noticed that a lotta cats here in Bmore tended to follow New York and Philly trends in fashion, and they did the same when it came to whips... whatever they were pushin' up there, they wanted to do the same down here... I get it, them shits was dope, but I was just never one to blindly follow.

"Quarter-key. Nine O's. Two-hunnid fiddy grams. Do I have to continue to break this shit down to ya *scrawny* ass?!?"

DUMMY.

We both laughed and headed to Royal Carry out in The Village for some chicken boxes. We could afford to eat wherever... The Palm, Phillips, Morton's... but sometimes you just want some shit from 'down tha way'. I swear Melvin has a tapeworm or something... the nigga eats and eats and *still* weighs only a buck twenty, soakin' wet with bricks in his pockets. I think that's one of the reasons why other niggas always fuck with him if they don't know him... or know *who* he's with... I tried to get him to hit the weight pile with me, but he always had some other shit to do... like puttin' a Gixxer600 engine in PureSport YZ250 frame... shit was a deathtrap, but was fast as a *muthafuckah!*

He took a *lotta* fools money with that one... l never understood why people raced him on that thing... all you had to do was *look* at it... the fuckin' fairing on it wouldn't even stay closed 'cause the engine was so big... that *alone* shoulda told you something was up with the bike, but niggas saw his skinny as on a YZ250 and thought 'I'mma carry *tha shit* out this nigga'... and then we ended up carryin' *their* dough.

We finished our chicken boxes, washing them down with half and halfs, trippin' off the phat ass youngins that came in. They knew that we were some 'money gettin' niggas', so they shook their asses just a little bit more than was necessary to just be walkin' into a damn store. Don't get me wrong, their bodies were bangin'... cute faces but they were *waaay* too young for us and besides it just bein' wrong and creepy, we'd already seen too many cats get caught up chasin' young pussy... that shit looks good right until shit gets thick and they start runnin' they mouth... to the police, the Feds, the competition... whoever will listen and give them something better than what they have right now. We watched 'the show' for a few minutes longer, then paid for their food too... this fucked 'em up 'cause they turned to us to holla and we told we'd get at 'em later-when we all knew that we wouldn't.

On the way to his car, Melvin mentioned some dude he wanted me to meet... Link, I think his name was, and then rolled out. He was on his way to see some new chick he was all in love with, so in my mind, the countdown to them breaking up had *already* begun. I went back home, got everything set up so I'd be ready to cook later, and then started wrenchin' on the Mustang. I had a race later on and needed to bolt up the slicks, change the nitrous jets, and a few other things. I'd heard the other Mustang I was set to race was runnin' 12's, but word was he was sprayin' too, so I knew I had to make some adjustments ...I figured between the 175 shot I was puttin' to it and me leavin' on his ass, I'd be okay. I'd already gotten some CAM-2 from the Sunoco on Reisterstown Rd... at $4 a gallon, it wasn't cheap, but 112 octane race fuel ain't supposed to be *economical*... besides, it was cheap insurance against the detonation that sprayin' nitrous can bring to an engine.

The 175 shot combined with the 400HP I had from the engine would be more than enough to fuck Kenny's '93 Cobra up... I had to give it to him, his car was slick as shit... bright red, black leather, Momo Quasar's with the 3" lip, bumpin' ass system... nice piece... and l was determined to *fuck* that pretty muthafuckah up with my '79, even if I had to blow my shit up doin' it! It looked like an '86 'cause I'd changed the front clip and tailights, as well as put in the Recaro seats from an '85, but the beauty was in the drivetrain... a '93 GT engine that I'd gotten from... well, let's just say I got the muthafuckah and leave it at that. Changed the cam, heads, re- flashed the computer, bigger injectors... bitch was *healthy,* but wasn't much too look at... which was fine, 'cause that made people sleep on it even more.

As I was countin' in my head how much of Kenny's money I was gonna take, my Nokia rang once, then twice, then three times. That was our code for how much was ready for pick up... in this case, 9 (multiply the number of rings times three), and I knew that whoever called on *that* phone was gon' be business related. I grabbed the keys to 'The Vault', the stash car I'd built for just such occassions and headed to the spot to get my 'cake mix'. As I drove the 1990 Toyota Corolla, down Edmondson Ave toward Hilton, I kinda chuckled to myself as I passed some corner niggas getting hemmed up by Baltimore City's finest... I don't know what was worse, the way they beat them boys *'just because'* everytime they pulled 'em up, or how easy the niggas made it to be pulled up in the first place... these cats was tennis shoe hustlers... they made enough for the latest Jordans, Jason Kidds... maybe a pair of Clarks and an outfit, and they were 'good'... then their stupid asses would fuck around and get locked up in the outfit they hustled all week to be able to cop... they made it *so obvious* as to what it was they were doin'... the light turned green; I left.

Cat piss. Normally, not a smell that you want to be greeted with when entering a room, but in this case, Calvin Klein's Obsession wouldn't have smelled as good... and these dickheads always had it... a Russian network that had distribution centers in Ohio, Vegas, New York, Atlanta, and Florida... if you had an 'in' with these cats, you were almost guaranteed to be gettin' money... their shit was just too good for you not to.

The only thing was, you had to know somebody to even get a beeper number for these dudes, and even that wasn't a guarantee that they'd sell to you... you actually had to like jive interview with them before they'd fuck with you... it wouldn't matter how much you were talkin', they researched the shit outta you before they even said the word 'coke' around you. But once you got on with 'em, and they saw that you were movin' shit lovely, that's when they started with the 'inside promotion' shit... Melvin wasn't sayin' that I should cop more just to be sayin it, he was just repeatin' what these cats were already 'strongly suggesting' that I do, and it was a suggestion I was very close to taking, but not on no consignment shit.

See, they'd front you whatever you wanted within reason of what they saw you already movin', one, two, shit... *fifty* bricks if you was like that, but you damn sure better have their dough when you supposed to, or they'd come after everybody you fuck with first, kill 'em slow in front of you, and then *you* last and *slower*. These muhfuckahs were Russian Mafia, and had the star tats and body counts to prove it... fuck 'em over if ya *wanna,* but it'd be the last thing you did before meetin' a painful demise.

I actually liked their business model though... some real old school 'as long as you do right by me, I'll do right by you' shit... something that this game has been getting twisted for a while now... ever since they got Rayful, niggas been goin hard for *real,* but in the wrong fuckin ways... too much wild cowboy shit followed up with reckless snitchin', and that brought all the wrong kinds of attention. I never understood exactly how you were supposed to collect a debt from a muhfuckah that you just killed, but that's what these youngin's was doin, and it was makin everything hot like shit.

Cat piss smell meant that the good Fishscale was on deck. This pearlescent colored, pungent smelling coke was the absolute *best* when it came to coppin' raw powder. Either Columbian or Peruvian, this shit always came back on the cook-up... and could take a hit, too. I wasn't one to B-12 my shit, but knowin' that it could take a healthy dose of it meant I could do my 'lil bakin' soda thing and bring back another 5 or 6 O's of that good shit... the shit that when it was done cookin', it looked kinda like dried pineapple... this was one of the reasons why I always made money... l cooked my own shit and made sure that the quality stayed high... sheeeiitt... the only thing higher than my quality was my customers.

"Carlos!" I hated when people that I wasn't cool with called me by my real name... and I was *not cool* with this muthafuckah *at all*. "Vladamir! What's the deal, comrade?" I never did like this Russian bastid... ever since my man Rick introduced us, it was just something about him that I didn't trust, even in this game where you really can't trust *anyone*... but Vlad... he was *especially* untrustworthy, but he was the gatekeeper for this shit, so I put emotions to the side and focused on money... you know... hustlah's creed and shit. Before he went in for 5 on some bullshit in Jersey, Rick told me that Vlad was a dickhead... I just didn't realize *how much* of a dickhead he'd end up bein'.

"So Carlos, you are coming back again to be picking up this eh...'lee-tull' sneeack, eh?" Fuck Vlad *and* his Eastern Bloc pronunciation of simple words such as 'little' and 'snack'. Vlad considered anything less than five bricks 'a snack' 'cause he was used to dealing with major players, and I wasn't that... yet... but his boss saw somethin' in me, because, well, he was *still* fuckin' with me... that and the fact that if you did the math, I was way more consistent than some of their bigger customers, 'cause I wasn't getting locked up or hot on the street for doin dumb shit... dumb shit that could fuck them up. I'd seen a couple dudes get cut slam the fuck off 'cause they were 'bout to bring heat to their doorstep. If you were *lucky,* they'd just stop selling to you... if not, they'd kill you and *everyone* in the upper levels of your organization 'just in case', because they didn't believe in 'loose ends'.

"Yeah mayne... little snack" is what I said, but in my mind I was tellin' him to *snack on deez* ..."When you see your boss, let him know I'm ready to have that talk with him" He hated when I made him messenger boy, which is exactly why I did it every chance I got... I knew that he knew better than to *not* give Vikktor any message that was sent to him... he never knew what Vikktor would consider important enough to kill for."What is it that you are wanting to be discussing with him?""Like I said" I replied..."it's a talk I need to have with *him,* not you". He handed me my groceries and muttered something in Russian... and I'm pretty sure the word 'nigger' was in there some-where ... that's why I be like 'fuck Vlad'.

Every time I used 'The Vault', I kinda smiled to myself... the way I set the stash spots up is nothing short of genius... you had to incorpo-rate the radio, wipers, reverse gear, and high beams in a specific, timed sequence ... if even one of 'em was a second off, the spot wouldn't pop; do it wrong twice, and the whole car locked down, spraying hydro-chloric acid on the contents of each spot. And speaking of the spots, they were made of ten-gauge steel lined with charcoal, cayenne pepper, and Juan Valdez's finest. I'd developed it as a paste that I spread on the walls between the spots... and I had six of 'em... ones for the product in both forms, ones for the tools, and ones for the scrilla. The car could have like a quarter mill worth of *whatever* in it and you'd park next to it at the Chapter Ill like some square ass nigga borrowed his mom's car to go to the club. I'd even installed a JDM spec engine in it to compen-sate for the extra weight... the only giveaway that it wasn't 'factory' was the paintjob, and even that was an inside joke... l had it painted pearl white... the same color of the Peruvian flake it was built to transport... I cracked my own damn self with that one.

Since the day was going pretty well, I knew it was only a matter of time before it'd get fucked up, and it did as soon as I got 'that' call... Shawn, my crazy fuckin girlfriend, was blowin' my phone up somethin' terrible. She knew I *generally* ignored her first call because, well, she *generally* ain't want shit... but this time, it was like four calls back to back, so I knew somethin' was up.

"S'up, what's tha deal?" I answered.

"You need to get the fuck home NOW! You been gone since *six this damn morning* and since you ain't bring ya black ass in until *four tha fuck* in the morning, ANNNDD ain't said TWO FUCKIN words to me, you need to come home, NOW!"

"*First* of fuckin' all," I replied, "I said *MORE* than two fuckin' words to you 'cause I told you to "ease up on the teeth" when you were suckin' my dick this morning at *four fifteen* in the morning because you swore all out I was out there fuckin, and ain't think my shit would get hard because of it."

Shawn *had* to prove her point and 'forgot' all that so she could continue to argue.

"You know what nigga?!? STAY THE FUCK WHERE YOU AT! I'm sure I can find some nigga that'll wanna stay up in this pussy without all the bullshit that *YOU* be givin' me... and ya dick game AIN'T that good *any* fuckin' way!!! **FUCK. YOU!**"

At this point, I'm figurin', 'cool', I got *way* more shit to be worried about than her bein' pissed with me *again*... I had my cake mix, and had just picked up $4700 from Eric... her talkin' that dumb shit just made it easier for me to take even longer to get over there.

And as far as my dick game was concerned, that was about the 489th time she'd said that shit, so apparently, it was in fact, *definitely* 'all that good'... I guess that race wit' Kenny's gon' have to wait a bit.

So I'm headed down 695 toward Randallstown ... I had a spot over there that I used to cook when I ain't wanna do that shit in one of the spots I had the Village... gotta change shit up to keep them bammas guessin'. I'm about to get off at exit 18, and I get flipped by an undercover. Normally, that kinda shit don't phase me, especially when I'm in The Vault, but I'm lookin' at this bitch and it ain't a regular Crown Vic... it's dumb clean and has the 'civilian package' that has the chrome grille to help it blend in better, and LED strobes... local radio cars don't equip their fleets like that because it costs too much, which means this is a fuckin' Fed.

I didn't know which one of the alphabet boys this was, so I go easy to the side of the road, lock all the spots, and 'produce my license and registration' 'cause I know that's what's comin' next. As I turn to the window, I catch the body of the driver in my mirror... and this bitch is *phat as all outdoors!!*

I knew this because even in that dumb ass 'blazer and slacks' look that all Feds be rockin', I could see this bitch looked she needed to be workin' at Eldo's, The Penthouse, Macombo's, or if she wanted to, *all fuckin' three*! By the time she got to my door, I was kinda hopin' she'd frisk me and ask about 'concealed weapons', but she didn't... what she *did* do was call me by name... which sent my shit soft with tha quickness ...

"Carlos Matthews", she said again, "You got some shit wit you, you know that right? But I like that... means you're serious about yours, and that means I'mma *definitely* get mine"

"Look," I replied, "I don't know what the fuck you talkin' bout, and how do you know my name, *officer* ...?"

I did that *officer* shit on purpose... l knew damn well she was a Fed, and she knew that *I* knew she was a Fed... but I also knew that Feds *hate* to be mistaken for regular cops... it's like callin' a Puerto Rican a Mexican... they just *don't like* that shit 'cause they think they're different enough for you to be able to tell the difference, and well, they're right.

"That's *AGENT* Ward, Carlos, and you might wanna stop trying to be cute because you're failing miserably. I pulled you over because, well, I *can, and* I know it's *fuckin' with you* that I did... l also wanted to let you in on a 'lil secret... you're about to owe me money, and a *lot* of it."

"The *fuck*", I quizzically inquired, "are you talkin' 'bout?!?"

"You'll find out soon enough... now run along and get that cake baked... mama needs a new pair of shoes... and a GSXR 750... so you need to get to work, *nigga!*" Then she turned and that phat ass got me rock hard again as I was watched her jiggle them cheeks all the way back to her car... the fact that I think I just got shaken down by a Fed meant absolutely nothing to me right then, because... right then... all I wanted to do was bend her over the hood of that car, and 'Fuck Tha Police'.

So now I got a problem... actually, quite a few problems ... fuckin' Feds not only know about me, but are tryin' to skinny up a nigga's pockets too! And how did she know about me bein' dirty as fuck?

I'm in The Vault!! *Nobody* knows about the secrets that it hides! Where tha fuck is this heat comin' from?? I know I'm on my shit, and Melvin is too... there weren't any others that knew enough to be a threat... shit, even Shawn's nutty ass (get it?) didn't know what I really did... she thought I was a bail bondsman, which was perfect because I could always be out and always be around 'criminals' without her asking why... well, *almost* always.

Anyway, I needed to figure out why I had Agent Booth in my muthafuckin' sleigh... and more importantly, how to resist the urge to

try and fuck her and just get rid of her. I didn't need this kind of attention, especially with me trynna go hard with Russians... the last thing
I needed was them thinking I was being *watched by,* or *working with*
the Feds. At that point, the smart half of me said 'Chill... cook later, go
get some pussy, call it a night', but the 'money gettin' nigga' half of me
said 'Fuck it; bake that cake, cut them slices and feed tha fuckin needy!'
Decisions, decisions ...

The water came to a boil quickly... this is why I liked gas stoves
over electric for this type shit, it was easier to control the flame, and it
just seemed to cook it more 'completely'. Electric stoves worked, but
they tended to scorch the coke in the process... I dunno... maybe it
was just me, but as far as I was concerned, gas was the only way to go
when you were cookin' up ready. I got my trusty Corning pot, dumped
the coke in, and got to controlling the flame... waited for it to 'snot up',
added my 'lil bakin' soda, worked the flame and added ice cubes to
shock it a bit... stirred and swirled a 'lil bit more and let that shit come
to rest with the flame off... the heat in the glassware would be enough
to do the rest, and besides, the cubes were doin' their thing as well. To
do this shit like I did it, the coke had to be doin' a 'hot/ cold, liquid
firming' type thing that unless you've done it, you wouldn't really get it
until you saw it... all I know is, this was how I would bring back everything plus like five or six extra... and still had the fiends on that 'one

hitter quitter' shit when they piped up... as far as cookin' *this* type shit, Julia Childs bitch ass ain't have *shit* on me.

I let the disc cool down about seven minutes in the pot before taking it out and puttin' it on some wax paper. I learned early on not to put it on paper towels, or even regular towels to dry it out; the paper and lint sticks to the ready and makes ya shit look all crazy... believe me... fiends don't want *nothin'* but *crack* in their *crack* and they'll try to beat you up on the price if they see lint or somethin' in there... you know, because they're concerned about their health when they're smokin' crack... fuckahs.

After letting it sit on the wax paper for about twenty minutes under a fan, I started cuttin' up; some for tha cat that called earlier, and some for other 'clients'. Most of the time, I did $20 pieces and some eight-balls for some of my 'paidster' customers ... these were the ones that I'd serve no matter how many times they called, 'cause each time they did, that was $180 in my pocket. I'd had this one chick call me for four of 'em in one night, so I started chargin' her $160... you would've thought I started chargin' her $10 she was so fuckin' grateful!

She was used to payin' $200 for some bullshit, and then had to deal with the ignorant muhfuckahs that served her like she was shit, so when she started coppin' from me, she got a beast product *and* some professional ass service... *any* reduction in the price was like butter for her... I swear, if I didn't get every bit of her Pargo's check, I know I got *most* of that muthfuckah!

After it was all said and done, after cuttin' up, I'd usually have between $3500 to $4200 in profit, give or take a few hundred...sometimes, when I wanted to stack even more, I'd sell the twenties for dimes just to piss them 'lil chicken box niggas off...I ain't give a fuck... none of 'em could fuck with my quality or quantity, and they all knew that I could shut they shop down just by showin' up...besides that, last I checked, *none* of 'em were bulletproof, and I *kept* guns... a *LOT* of guns. Run up on me if ya wanna... I'd have you touchin' *everything* in the room...and It wasn't like I ain't have a hand game, I was nice wit my mitts, but since nobody actually tussled anymore, I'd have been a fool to not keep that wit' me...I was the Bmore Tony Starks 'cause I kept that iron, man...get it?

In fact, the only times I wasn't strapped was when I was on campus... I actually felt jive safe there 'cause at that point, nobody knew what I did... once I *left* Howard's grounds, however, that warm and fuzzy feeling immediately left. I was going there for graphic design seein' as how I'd always been told I could draw and I figured it would be the easiest way to get a degree. I was honestly surprised that I got accepted because I really didn't take the admissions process seriously. It wasn't that I wasn't 'smart enough'; I'd carried a high B average throughout high school, and if I'd shown up more, it'd been much higher. I figured out around 10th grade that all you really had to do is show up for the 'important tests' and turn in the 'important papers', and the rest of the time you could just chill... which is exactly what I did... by the time I was a junior, I had a car which meant I was showin' up for school less and less while at the same time becoming more and more popular... go figure.

By the time I graduated high school, I was on my second car, and my first taste of the drug game. My buddy Chris was movin' powder and was getting paid... knots of $5000 or more were the regular for him, which in '89, was something to talk about... especially since he wasn't on the corner. Workin' strictly off his beeper, he had dough, jewels, clothes, and a bangin' ass Amigo when everybody else was still fuckin' wit Suzuki Samurais and Mitsubishi Monteros... muhfuckah had the 16" Riken swirl wheels on it, Alpine pull- out, Bazooka basstubes and he'd upgraded the top to a custom canvas version... shit was *on point.*

Anyway, he wanted me to do a run for him, but that never happened ... which was fine with me 'cause I didn't wanna get up that early anyway. He was talking about bein' on the road at like 5 in the morning to go to New York. He was kickin' out for gas and food, plus $300 for my trouble... yeah, I didn't know any better back then, so I guess that's another reason why it was good the trip never happened... but what *did* happen was he had me help him bag up some powder.

These *tiny* ass bags were goin' for $10 according to him, and he had a rack of 'em. He gave me a couple to do with what I wanted, and you couldn't *tell* me I wasn't Tony Montana! I didn't have anyone to sell 'em to, didn't even know *who* to sell 'em to, but dammit, I had some coke, which for some reason 'empowered' me. I knew that if I sold enough of this stuff, there wouldn't be too much that I *couldn't* have. It wasn't like we were poor... well, not anymore, but the memories of me not havin' much back home in Cleveland were still fresh in my mind.

We were years removed from E. 55, Quincy, St. Claire, and a gang of other fucked up streets that make up some of the grimiest parts of East Cleveland where I was born and raised. You know what though? For as rough as it was back home, I never 'felt scared'...it was '*just home*' to me and since it was all I ever knew, I guess I didn't know enough to be scared...plus, as with any thorough area, that fear shit don't fly too well back home...I'd seen a lot and been through a lot back in Cleveland, but the funny thing was, I didn't see my first shooting victim until we 'bettered ourselves' by moving to Baltimore. Me and my boy Sean were up on Johnnycake Middle's baseball field, and outta nowhere, this dude got shot for his mini bike... dude got shot in the shoulder and the cat that shot him, left him leakin' on the field and just rode off on his bike like "*And*??!!"

I guess all that kinda crystallized as I looked at what was at thetime, a relatively worthless amount of coke... but for some reason, those two bags kinda 'inspired' me to go down a path that I knew I shouldn't, but I also knew I'd be damn good at it... funny how some things work out that way.

So I've got these two bags of coke, now what?

Not a damn thing, that's what. Didn't sell 'em, didn't give 'em away, didn't dip in 'em to see what the hype was about, though I did think about it, but the fear of instant addiction prevented from ever doing so...ever...so what did I do?

Forgot about 'em and ended up washing them in a pair of jeans... so much for my Scarface dreams. I wasn't even pressed at that point... the charge I got from havin' it was enough for me at that point... l still had my job at Giant, so it wasn't like I *had* to sell drugs, I just really *wanted* to sell drugs... fast forward to the time I started goin' to Howard, I had a decent clientele built up... I was stayin' in The Village where I rented the basement of my boy Corey's house, right on the corner of Woodington and Rokeby. Lotta pride in EV... when it got cold out, 'lil niggas had WAR & RAW airbrushed on their bombers to rep the corner, but I think it was mostly 'cause the shit sounded cool... I guess it was kinda clever flippin' the street names into an acronym ... right until niggas started getting fucked up and shot at for havin' 'the wrong street' on they bombers and now Bmore... is 'jus lyke Compton'.

Anyway, I still had my job at Giant, but hustlin' soon pushed that all the way to the side... I was up all night rollin' rocks and had 8:30A classes at Howard... it got to the point where I couldn't 'fit a job into my schedule', so after 5 years at Giant, I took a leave of absence under the FMLA... you know, just in case this drug dealin' thing didn't work out, I wanted to have a job to come back to... I figured if I couldn't make it *'happen* happen' in the 6 months that FMLA gave you, it just wasn't meant to be... then... I quickly found out that it was *very much* meant to be.

Without the pesky job in the way, I could focus more on school and more importantly to me at the time, movin' more shit. I was breakin' down half ounces like every other day, and since I was doin' it night shift, I was able to sell light bags (shake) for full price... which further increased my profit, 'cause a lot of those were 'books' I damn sure didn't count! It wasn't long before I was movin' O's and at the time, thought it was all the money in the world.

I didn't really need much and had scraped by for so long on so little that havin' any extra dough seemed like a lot, so when I started havin' consistent high four to low five digit profits, I thought I was a rich man... it was only *me* at the time, so all the profit came back to me *and only me!* Like I said, I didn't need or want for much, so me bein' able to get the new Larry Johnson's, a Cadillac on switches, and keep a high 3 to low 4 digits in my pocket as 'walk around' money made me feel like I was runnin' shit because, well, in the small pond that I was in, I actually was... or so I thought.

I continued to bag my shit up, filling bag after bag with death metered out into convenient, 12 min. intervals... the more the fiends *loved* me, the more I *hated* me, but if I didn't sell it to 'em, they were just gon' buy it from someone else anyway, so I finished baggin' and got ready to pack up.

"Ay yo! You gon' meet this dude or what? The boy Link got Sandtown on lock, but he 'bout to lose it 'cause he can't stay on... you gettin' that good Russian shit by as much as you want... you need to hit Link off and let *dat* nigga work for *you!*" Melvin made a good point... shit, he made *several* good points 'cause at the end of the day, this one man show shit was startin' to wear on me. "Set it up," I said..."let me know the time and place and I'll be there... I'll be late, but I'll be there." We both laughed because we knew to never show up on time for this kinda thing... you were either way early or way late. This made settin' you up for tha 'okie-doke' a bit more difficult because whoever you were meetin' didn't know exactly when you were actually comin'... it was ignorant and mad unprofessional, but in these circles... it was perfect business etiquette.

We met at LakeTrout... Reisterstown Rd. was a high traffic spot that I was pretty sure this dude wouldn't try anything at The Roost, and if he did, I knew I had enough dudes there kick this nigga off tha planet if need be, plus a police station was right next door so niggas tended to act friendly at least until they got up the street... I was expec-tin' the worst, but he was mad cool. Link was in the Navy and got a dishonorable for hustlin'... they couldn't get a conviction but they *could* give his ass a Double-D to make sure that he couldn't use the Navy as a reference. It was fucked up, but hey, that was the military... you do it their fucked up way or they fuck up *your* way... I learned that much from my father... the shit he told me he went through in Vietnam was enough for me to *never* look at joining the service... and I actually wanted to as a kid... I wanted to be a fuckin' SEAL, but since I can't open my eyes under water, that shit got x'd out real quick... then I wanted to be a Ranger... Special Forces and shit... then I wanted to be in the Air Force until I found out how much math you gotta know to fly jets... in the end, my father told me how none of that shit mattered when you were 'in country' becuase the training is only gonna get you so far and that no matter what branch you choose, you gotta turn into a monster to survive or you ain't comin' home. He told me about the crazy ways people got killed over there, and how human life was mad cheap… seein death every second of every minute of hour of every day, getting high as fuck to try to numb the pain, then realizin' that you can't ever get 'high enough' to numb Hell, which was what you were in, but now you got an addiction to some shit that'll take a lifetime to shake… then, after goin through all that, the country you was riskin' ya ass for and seein friends get blown the fuck up for, spits on you when you get off the plane… like, literally… hawks up, and *spits* on you… yeah… after that, I was like *fuck* the service. I would later learn that the service wasn't the root of the problem, it was the country, but I digress.

Anyway, we ordered two regulars and half & halfs then proceeded to talk business, with Link wasting no timne and mincing no words.

"Melvin said you was dat nigga to know, wassup? I'm tryin' to flood tha block but these niggas I be dealin wit be on some straight *bullshit*… sometimes they package on point and sometimes they not… shit, sometimes they ain't got shit *at all* and a nigga gotta turn fiends away… and I HATE turnin fiends away!" Ah yes. The ebb and flow of supply and demand.

"Ay yo, if you serious, I can keep you on Link, but it ain't gon' be cheap, and you gon' have problems... tha kinda shit I'mma supply you makes tha local niggas '*up-tha-fuck set*', ya hear me? I sent some fiend to cop from down yo way... the bottles is full, but it's still that oatmeal looking shit that everybody from the Village to Yale Heights be pumpin'... it sells, but only because whether or not y'all know it, *all* ya'll be coppin' from the same 2-3 dudes... and they *all* got bullshit that's been stepped on more than the Burger King mat down Mondawmin Mall... I'm comin wit that *Fishscale* with no more than a two on it when it'll take a six and *still* be a killer... and them fiends gon' happily pay you $20 for what them other niggas sellin' as dimes... I'm just sayin', niggas gon' be feelin' a certain kinda way... you ready for that?""Man **FUCK** them niggas!! Ain't NO way they gon' stop my fuckin flow... just put me on and I'll do the rest, no doubt!"

Link's response was perfect. This could be good for me... his sense of pride and highly competitive nature had served him well for all the wrong reasons and the mix of his drive and my product was the perfect recipe for us to get *dumb* paid."My Glock *STAY tha* fuck ready... you get me that good shit 'Los and word bond, I'mma get us paper like you ain't NEVER seen!!" I had to admit, I liked his enthusiasm ... it reminded me of a slightly younger, way more rage fueled, version of me.

"Cool... 'cause if you don't have my money Link... I will give you one chance to make it right... but know this... there WILL NOT be a second chance. I ain't trynna hear this person or that person fucked up, got knocked, got robbed (a Bmore favorite as far as excuses), or NONE of that shit... I'm working with *you,* so the weight is on *you and you* alone."

"Los, look... I'm not tryin' to fuck you over... as long as you get that good shit, the money ain't gon' be a problem" After a bit more back and forth,we exchanged numbers and went our separate ways. I already knew I was gon' fuck wit him, but I wasn't gon' let *him* know that. So now, I have what could amount to be what I was finding that I really needed... a workforce... and *this* workforce already came with a leader and a paying demographic; this shit was about blow up for *real.*

All in all... it was a pretty good meeting... I prolly shoulda listened to Melvin earlier about meetin' Link... oh well... live and learn. Shit! I'm reminiscin' and need to finish packin' this shit up so I can hit these cats off... I hit my regulars off with their packages since I'd already collected any loose money that was still roamin' the streets... I learned early that you needed to get your money before providin' the re-up for people... you may not know this, but people tend to *not* pay you money owed for *old* drugs if you give them *new* drugs *first...* go figure. I then hit Link off with his first package from me, a couple of ounces that I knew would piss him off since he was expecting a lot more. I needed to see how soon he could move this and more importantly, how serious would he take it... see, to me, it didn't matter if it was an eight ball or a quarter-key, it ALL needed to be taken seriously... plus, I needed time to get some more product, so it'd all work out if he took it seriously.

He apparently took it seriously then a muthafuckah, because he called me back in an hour with the money and the need for more. Since he'd passed the first test, I made sure I had a brick at the stash house for cookin' up later, then I went home. I was already prepared for her stupid ass, but Shawn was gone... unfortunately, it wasn't for good and she'd returned on some bullshit.

I'd just gotten to sleep when Hurricane Shawn touched down. Liberty Gardens wasn't exactly what you call a 'quiet' apartment complex, but even by its standards, Shawn was loud as shit. She was bitchin' about somethin' or the other (water bein' wet, the fact that cats meow, the sun rising in the East or some other shit...), and I did what I normally did... try my best to ignore her, question why I was still with her, then remind myself that 'oh yeah, it's because the pussy is a bomb', and because I'd caught her fresh off an abortion when I'd met her, she was still lactating... what can I say? Squirty titties are a turn-on for me.

The problem was that this time, it wasn't enough and I actually responded to her dumb ass. See, Shawn was the type of female that thought the more you abused her, the more you cared for or loved her. Since I'd never been one to beat on women (other than the pussy), she thought that I didn't care for or about her, which was ironic, because at one point I really thought I loved her. I think that like a lot of women, it was this 'lack of a loving male role model' that helped make her that way... her father was abusive to her mother and since her mother stuck around for the hits, she saw that as an expression of 'love'... that pretty much insured that she'd end up a stripper, or getting pregnant by her own cousin... or both.

Okay, it was actually *only one*... and she was never a stripper.

She said she thought 'no one will love you like a family member' (really... that's what she said), so I guess letting your cousin cum inside you makes sense when you put it like *that*.

Let me repeat that to be sure that it marinates correctly... she not only *fucked* her cousin, knowing *full well* that it was her cousin, but she also *let him nut inside of her* thinking 'this is okay, because it's family, and no one loves you like family'.

Now, in *my* defense, let me remind you that as previously mentioned, *the pussy was a bomb,* and I have a thing for lactating titties... I'm a freak and I'm ok with that.

So the argument gets louder, the hunter green kitchen accessories are flyin like crazy, and then... the punches start bein' thrown... and lemme tell ya... this bitch had a *nasty* right... the shit was damn near indefensible. Now, I know all you 'thorough niggas' are readin' this and goin'"I wish a bitch would swing on me, I'll knock that bitch tha fuck out, wake her up, then, *knock her bitch ass out again!*"

And to you thorough niggas, I would remind you that the only thing on women I beat is the pussy, so clearly, I was at a loss in this fight and she knew it... l ended up catchin' one of those rights I mentioned earlier. It just grazed me, but because of the argument earlier, my mouth is dry and so are my lips... so now I got a busted lip. On top of that, this bitch pulls my HK USP . 40 on me... and pulls the trigger. For whatever reason, there were no bullets in the mag or chamber, but then again, it was one that I hadn't been carrying for awhile, so I guess it made sense... truth be told, I had quite a few guns and actually forgot I owned the damn thing.

I know, I know... but walk with me, I'm goin' somewhere with this.

The neighbors called the police and Shawn goes *off...* she's tellin' one-time that I beat on her, that I cuss her ass out all the time, and as if that shit wasn't enough... she fuckin' tells them that I sell drugs and that I have a gun on me right now. Now, if you've never dealt with one-time, the *LAST* thing they wanna hear is that someone besides them has a gun that they don't know about.

Carlos, meet the concrete, concrete, meet Carlos' face, chest, stomach, and thighs.

With tha quickness, these muhfuckahs 'detain' me with the help of the fuckin sidewalk and find out that the bitch was only half right... I *did* sell drugs, but had none and no gun on me at the time... lucky me!

Once they were satisfied that I was armed with only the ones attached to my shoulders and hands (get it?), they noticed my bloody lip. This, in addition to the fact that nothing Shawn said to this point was panning out had them tell her to be quiet, and they started listen to me... I told 'em take a look at my fuckin' face.

Now, sure, that could've come from them earth slammin me to the concrete, but then they would have had to acknowledge that they earth slammed me to the concrete... which they weren't gonna do... so now, it 'made sense' that Shawn may have popped me before they got there, and I ain't have to do or say shit other than 'look at my fuckin' face'; it ended up bein' a 'no write-up' call and they left after givin' both of us warnings... verbal, non-documentable, warnings.

So, back to all you 'thorough niggas' that woulda 'whupped her ass', ya thorough ass woulda been eatin' cold burgers in a bullpen somewhere locked up on a domestic. I looked at her, smirked a bloody smile and went to go prep this shit for Link... I'd have to deal with her trying to murder me a bit later... there's a lot of dollars out here and I'm tryin' to collect the whole fuckin' set.

I hit my spot and got my 'Chef-D-R Boy' on so I could hit Link off. I told him earlier that I needed to see him about something and he knew exactly what I meant. I cooked up the brick, dried it out, then took my extra off the top to pass out once I hit Link off. I had my . 380, a . 40, and a Mossberg with me... just in case.

I pulled up to in The Vault and told Link to get in so I could get him goin'. For whatever reason, this nigga smelled like he bathed in Egyptian Musk, and the shit was seriously clashin' wit' my Morning Fresh air fresheners ... anyway, we drove to a 'safe area' so I could hit him off with the product. I broke out the digital scale, zeroed it out in front of him, and proceeded to weigh out 1028 grams of that good shit. I threw in an extra ounce for a couple of reasons... one was because I'd cheffed up close to an extra quarter brick *anyway* so it ain't mean shit to me and two, I was only chargin' Link for a brick and an extra ounce *definitely* meant something to him. That couple few grand that he could pocket off that ounce would come in handy once I needed a 'favor' down the line... and by taking the 10-28, he already accepted the fact that he'd owe me. Add to that the fact that on the strength of Melvin, I was frontin' Link, so I was already makin' a front-tax off his ass anyway, so believe me, ya boy wasn't losin' out.

Since I was getting them powder thangs for about $30Gs, I could front bricks of ready for $40Gs and get no complaints... if you had the clientele to need a brick, but couldn't get the $50Gs that some other niggas was chargin' for bullshit, 'owin' me $40Gs was a bargoin... add to that the fact that I ain't front many people, and it really wasn't that big of a deal. I made at least $1OGs off each brick of ready that I fronted, on top of the extra that I cheffed up on each one... plus, I still had a couple spots that I ran that weren't ready for bricks yet, but still made some okay dough... I was far from needy by not bein' greedy.

About 3 days went past and Link needed some more. Then another 3 days, and another, and another, blah, blah, blah. I was makin' at least $30Gs a week off Link alone, and while it wasn't much to the people that I ran with, it was *more* than enough for me... remember... I ain't need much in the first place and prolly could've quit after a few weeks of havin' Link on board... but like most intelligent dummies, I didn't do what I *should've* done.

Everything was goin' smooth... again... too smooth, so I should've known it was gon' be some shit... and I was right... l just didn't know at the time, *just how right.*

Melvin was buggin' me about some rap cats that he was tryin' to get put on... they were some local niggas that went to Morgan and were supposed to be jive nice... Melvin was their engineer/ producer/ promoter/ whatever else they needed to get noticed. He said they were openin' for some other unknown muhfuckahs at The Palladium. I told him I'd try to see what I could do, knowin' full well I wasn't goin to no show... and Melvin should've known too seein' as how l ain't fuck wit crowds like that... l didn't like bein' no where where I couldn't keep an eye on everybody. Even when I *would* go to clubs, it would be just that; I would 'go to the club', as in, I'd meet in the parkin' lot or some-thin'...'cause when you mix liquor wit a rack of niggas showin' off for the tackhead bitches in the club, it's only a matter of time before you get pulled into somebody else's bullshit, and I wasn't trynna go outta here on a humble.

The 'bullet with your name on it' isn't the one you need to be worried about, it's the bullets that just have *occupant* written on them that'll fuckin' kill you *every* time.

Shawn was actually acting human for some reason, so we'd gone out to eat. I gotta say, when she wasn't bein a complete fuckin' maniac, Shawn was a *beast!* She was kinda cinnamon hued and sorta favored Jada a 'lil bit in the eyes, but was *phat den a muhfuckah*... nice titties and mo' ass than a donkey... plus, when I met her she was on the tail end of an abortion (you know... becuase her cousin knocked her up), so she was always horny as shit and tha titties stayed leaky. I ain't mind at all 'cause me bein the freak that I am, bein able to squeeze those plump ass tits and have milk squirt out was a fuckin turn-on that I didn't even know *did it* for me until it happened! So, I say all that to say, that even though she was certifiable most of the time, I still remembered *other* qualities that kept bringin' me back... what can I say? I'm a man and don't always think with the correct head.

We got back home, chilled for a 'lil while (fucked), and I told her I had to go work on a skip before her nutty-mode inevitably kicked in again. I figured it'd give me some time to check on my spots, see how Melvin's show went, and get back to get some sleep for my morning class. Since I wasn't gon' be 'supa-dirty', I left The Vault parked and took the Caddy.

I really liked the Cadillac... out of all my cars, it was the one I was most proud of... it was an '83 Fleetwood Brougham ... *coupe*. This is important to a car guy because most of the Broughams made were sedans, so to have a coupe was cool, and rare as well. It had the same wheelbase or length as a sedan, which meant the doors were long as shit!

I thought that was cool because I was never really a sedan kinda guy... four door cars just looked kinda crazy to me, unless they were cars that I couldn't see myself buying at the time, like an S Class or a 7. When I bought it, niggas down the way thought I was crazy... while everyone else was rimming up an Ack Coupe or Benz, I was in an 'old man Caddy'... I'd been looking for an older car for a while to replace my '69 Lincoln MarkIII,so when Melvin had told me about a two-door Caddy, I was damn sure interested... when I found out it was aFleet-wood Brougham, I *had* to have it.

Plus, I had seen one done up in that Warren G. video for Regulators ... that candy paint, white top, white interior, chrome D's... these Baltimore niggas weren't gon' know what hit 'em! My car game was always jive tight on the speed tip 'cause a nigga kept a 5. 0 that ran like a muhfuckah... but wit' this Caddy... l was gon' be on some *other* shit.

Melvin and I drove out to Elksburg to take a look at the car and it was *tight as fuck!* The older dude sellin' it was the original owner... he'd bought it for his family to take trips in, and stopped driving it about three months ago... but even still, for it to be an '83, the 27,000 miles on it wasn't shit for a 12 year old car! Dude wanted $4K, but I wanted to leave with a 'lil pocket change, so I offered him $3K cash. He was kinda hesitant 'cause he knew how nice the car was, but I also knew that it whatn't gon' be a lotta people checkin' for the car flashin' 300 ten dollar bills in his face... I learned that from Don King... he said in his book somethin' to the effect that if you show a boxer a check for $1OK, he *may* be excited to sign a contract, but if you pull out $5K in fives, that *same* boxer will sign the *same* contract... in his own blood... cash in hand is a *muthafuckah!*

I gave dude the $3K and drove off in the 'new to me' Cadillac.

I didn't have the car two weeks before I was headed to Miami... l was readin' some Lowrider magazines and figured 'why not?' Even though Billy and Kevin over at Rim Source were doin' hydraulics, I thought it'd be cool to drive to Red's Hialeah in Miami and have them do it... they did a gang of magazine cars, and everybody that was *anybody* in the lowrider world had either entire Red's hydraulic systems, or at least had some of their parts... plus, I was bored and wanted to see how fast I could get down there, get it done, and get back.

Two days and $3700 later, I was back in Baltimore with a 'Red's Hydraulics equipped' Cadillac, and some cool ass pics of the car when I stopped at 'South Of The Boarder' on the way back to Maryland. I called Kevin as soon as I got back and had him order me a set of chrome Roadstars wit' the gold nipples and knock-offs... they were along the same line as Daytons without the long ass wait to have 'em built. I built a box with two Cerwin Vega's in it, fiberglassed the doors, threw an Orion 2250 in there for good measure and *just like that...* I had one of the tightest cars in Bmore ... it had gotten to the point where muhfuckahs would know *the car* before they knew me!

Seriously ... I'd be talkin' to some random dude at the barber shop or somewhere and they'd be tellin' me about a 'pretty ass Cadillac that was laid on the ground' or a 'bad ass Caddy that was parked kinda funny'... sometimes I would leave the car 'locked up' with the front in the air, or leaned to the side... but mostly I just pancaked it... and that was only because I was so used to doin' it to avoid gettin' a boot on it (I have a few unpaid tickets) when I parked on campus... Howard University's parking enforcement dickheads couldn't get a boot on that bitch if they *life* depended on it!

Then I got the call that pulled me off of 'Memory Lane' and brought my ass back to the present wit tha quickness. It wasn't the fact that Derrick was calling me... shit, Derrick's like a father figure to

Melvin and I, so we all talked on the regular; it was just something weird about the way he was blowin' my phone up... like he was pressed or somethin'.

Ever since I met Derrick, he was always cool... real laid back despite everybody in The Village and beyond knowin' him. He's got a vibe that commands admiration and respect at the same time... that whole 'women want him and men want to be him' type shit.

When I first 'met' him, it was before I was livin' the structured life... I had this older 5.0 Mustang that I thought was the fastest shit on the street, so when I pulled up on this burgundy Mercedes 190 at the light on Rte. 40 where Chi-Chi's is, I thought '*This* nigga!' The car was jive tight though... burgundy metallic, AMG kit, BBS, Orion sticker on the back window and some 'Music Mart II' shit on the front. I had only seen AMG Benzes in magazines, and honestly thought. .. ain't no hustlin' ass niggas gon' actually *buy* one... most niggas were more concerned with style over performance to spend *that* kinda money on a car that while it looks good, the price you were payin' for it was for the shit that you *couldn't* see... suspension, exhaust, engine and fuel system management ... *that* kinda shit. Dude drivin' had some Cazal's on... not the ones like DMC was rockin', he had one the ones that Hammer had wit' the 'lil gold shit between the lenses and the arms... big ass 30mm herringbone,

Sergio Tachini crinkle sweatsuit and this heavy lookin' gold bracelet. I figured, 'this nigga got *dough,* but ain't *no way* I'mma let a kitted-up, fake AMG Baby Benz whup my ass!' My shit wasn't pretty, but it *ran...* fuck dat pretty muthafuckah next to me... when that light falls, I'ma bust dat ass!

Unfortunately, the only ass that got busted was *mine.*

The light fell, and all I saw was a cloud of smoke fire outta the AMG tipped exhaust that from the sound of it, did not know the meaning of catalytic converters nor resonators, that turned that burgundy bastid into a vanishing point of European performance... yeah... this nigga was clearly on some *other* shit.

Turns out that not only was it a *real* AMG... it was a real AMG with a Calloway turbo... damn shame I wouldn't find that out until later... if I'd known, I could've saved myself some embarrassment that would end up bein' jokingly 'used against me' for the duration of our friendship. It also turned out that the driver wasn't hustlin' shit but car stereo, records, bus passes, and lottery tickets... Music Mart II was a shop in Edmondson Village that sold all that shit and Derrick owned it. He had hustler money *without* actually havin' to hustle... imagine *that.*

Like I said, I found all of this out after 'after the fact', because I'd actually been there before to buy tapes... I just never took notice to the name... and I *damn* sure didn't know about the stereo shit they did 'in the back'. I'd pulled up to the front of the shop one night when I saw this lowered Toyota extended cab SR-5, V6 pickup... again, burgundy in color, but it had these stripes and shit on it... chrome American Racing Hammers, 50 series tires... and sittin next to it was a blue B2200 that was just as low, and just as hooked up... it was sittin' on Centerlines, and while the particular style was usually at home on cars, they actually *worked* on this truck.

The shop was 'officially' closed, but they were hangin' out and I figured I'd stop and say somethin'... I told them both that their trucks was fresh, got a closer look at the trucks, and was blown slam away... the blue one was still bein' worked on and even though it was still basically a wood frame, you could see how the center console was gonna come together ... it had a space for a TV, switch panel, radio.. *and* it had a fuckin' Ratical Top targa conversion! The bed had a hard-cover, but underneath were speakers, amps, and extra batteries, and it had a pass-through cut in it so the bass could travel from the bed into the cab... the owner's name was Bruce, and while he looked like he'd smack you as soon as look at you, he was really a cool dude... he was a gearhead from way back that fucked wit' cars and bikes, but was mainly into bikes now. The burgundy one was Derrick's and the area behind the two front seats was a wall of speakers... at this time it was six 15 inch woofers, but I would later learn that at one time, it had four 18's in it.

Sure, it had some other speakers in the doors, but having never seen *that many* speakers in anything *in real life,* let alone that many *big ass* speakers in real life I didn't *care* about the doors and shit!

I walked my amazed ass back to my car impressed like shit... these cats were legally getting hustlah type money... sure, Derrick had the store and from the looks of Bruce's work shirt, he did something at Russel Mazda... but if you just saw 'em out there chillin', youd'a swore they was movin' them *thangs!*

I started hangin' out at the store shortly after that, first as a customer buyin' amps for my system and even havin' an alarm installed... I'd bought it down the Convention Center's electronic show... I could wire up amps, speakers, and radios, but I'd never done an alarm so I figured I'd get Music Mart II to do it.

Little did I know I'd end up hangin' out in the back shop with Pro, the Installation Manager, while he did the work. I ended up not being able to get that alarm installed because Pro said that there were some other parts I needed that I really couldn't afford to get right then, but what I *did* get was invited by Pro to hang out and learn more about car stereo... and if *that* wasn't cool enough, Derrick had co signed my potential as well. There was also this skinny dude that was there all the time... he didn't 'work' there, but he was always around Derrick... that skinny dude's name is Melvin... the same Melvin that I would end up hustlin' with.

I'd showed him the trunk of my Mustang to get an idea of what I neededto do... he told me to clean up the wires that looked, as he put it, 'like a bowl of spaghetti'... since I had an Orion 280GX that I bought form him as part of the system, he also told me that I couldn't be rollin' around with 'high dollar equipment lookin' *raggedier than a bowl of yat gaw mein!'... but* for what I had (amp, Bazooka bass tube, and some 6x9's with an Alpine radio), he said it sounded pretty good. I took him at his word because really, while this dude didn't have no reason to lie, he also was pushin' what I found out was the loudest truck in Baltimore City at the time... I wasn't no threat to his shit and he could've easily been like *'take dat bamma ass shit down the road',* but he didn't...l thought that was cool 'cause I'd met people with a lot less goin' on that tried to carry muhfuckahs. I went from hangin' out at the shop to actually workin' there... shit... at one point, I was workin there, at Giant, goin' to Howard, *and* slangin' all at the same time... you can't tell me *shit* about 'time management'! Derrick was always that dude that kept me from goin' *too* far... he'd even prevented me pickin' up my Mustang from the transmission shop from becomin' an attempted murder charge.

Long story short, I'd taken it in for an estimate, and got called later that day bein told I owed them $800 because they went ahead and fixed the car. I told them I was comin' to get my car, but I was also takin' one of the 'shop mascots' with me... a Llama . 45 that was gonna be my insurance policy... see, the transmission shop was run by some 'good 'ol boys' and was just far enough down Ritchie Highway for me to be 'concerned' about how this shit would play out... but Derrick being Derrick, fuckin' frisked me before I left the shop... he found the gun (wasn't like I was *hiding* it), took it from me, and saved two crackers from getting shot, aswell as me from being locked up for some *years*. Once I started hustlin' 'for real', Derrick never judged me, but I always knew that he didn't '100% approve'.

Come to think of it, he was never really thrilled about Melvin *or* me hustlin' because he saw so much more potential in us for other shit... Melvin with music and cars and me with my artwork and, well, cars... but enough about that, back to the call.

"S'up Duurrrick!" I hadn't talked to him in a few, so it was good to hear from him... until I heard, "Whassup man... hey, are you drivin' right now?" I quizzically replied "Yeah, why; you need me to come past there?""Nahh," he replied, "I need you to pull over real quick though." I told I'd pulled over even though I really hadn't and said "Okay... what's goin' on?"

"Melvin's gone... he's dead, man."

I almost ran into the rocks that had a Range Rover on them at Frankel Range Rover on Reisterstown Rd.

"WHAT THA FUCK HAPPENED???" I screamed into the phone, really pulled over at this point. Derrick went on to tell me that he'd been shot outside of his apartment building... something about him taking the trash out and getting shot in the process, which, in Edmondson Village wasn't exactly an abnormal occurrence ... but the fact that the chick he'd fallen in love with this time was kinda shady had all of us thinkin' she had somethin' to do with it... especially since she would end up disappearing before the nigga was even in the ground.

"Derrick... what... naahhh man... Mel can't be dead... I just talked to his ass *yesterday* about hookin up for the concert *tonight!!!*"

"I know man... I talked to him about that too". Derrick's answers unfortunately did nothing but create more questions. I got back to the Village and talked to my man Corey... he said he'd actually seen Melvin laid out and didn't even know it was him... he was so fucked up from the gunshot that the only way Corey knew it was him was because of Melvin's white beeper.

Melvin was like, the *only* cat that could pull off wearin' a fuckin white beeper... we used to joke the shit out of him about it, but it was mainly because we were all jealous that we could never keep a white beeper, well, *white.*

"Yo" Corey said with his distinct Baltimore drawl, "That's fucked up how they did Mel, man... whoever did that shit ran the fuck up on 'em, and just laid his ass out... whatn't no gettin' away from that shit man..."

"Did anybody see who did it?" I asked, already knowing the answer was not only"naw", but"*hail* naw".

"Naww, c'mon son... you know ain't nobody gon' say shit 'round here... even if they *did* see dat shit they ain't trynna get caught up in no murder case."

The next few weeks were really bad... we had the funeral and like I said earlier, the bitch never showed up... Melvin's father acted like it wasn't 'no big deal' that his son was dead.

Days before the funeral and not too long afterward, Baltimore City homicide was questionin' everybody, but they were just goin' through the motions... because of Melvin's prior association with some money gettin' niggas that caught and beat murder cases along the way, they just chalked it up as another drug related murder... which is to say they ain't 'investigate' worth a fuck... it would be up to us to find out who did it and 'handle it'.

Link was movin' shit like an epileptic on a toilet... Melvin's death didn't slow him down in the least... it was kinda cold since we were all cool, but that's Link... shit, it was actually an enviable trait... as much as I tried, with certain things I just couldn't 'remove myself' from the situation...I couldn't always 'not give a fuck', and in this business, giving a fuck when it ain't your turn could get you killed.

Going to class was real fucked up during this time... I would show up, park the Caddy in some ridiculous ass way (tilted to one side, pancaked, etc.) that would hopefully prevent it from gettin' a boot put on it and try to focus on *that* stress to distract me from Melvin getting killed. Whole time, getting' a boot was a real concern for me because I swear, D. C. parking enforcement had it out for me ever since I took one of their boots off of my Mustang... the cop I lived next door to at the time said it'd be a Federal offense since it happened in the City, so I had to drive back, position the boot on it and call parking enforcement to come back and 'remove' it... the nigga that showed up was jive huffin' 'cause he could tell it had been removed, but it wasn't shit he could do about it 'cause it wasn't damaged ... anyway, like I said, class was real fucked up... l didn't want to be there for obvious reasons, but money was paid, and goin' to the A building talkin' 'bout 'I need a break, can I have some of my money back' was NOT gonna happen.

I made the best of my situation... I'm a college student trynna get a degree so that I can eventually 'get a good job with benefits'... while at the same time controlling a pretty fuckin' lucrative coke operation that ironically enough, afforded me the ability to *not* have, or *need* a 'good job with benefits' ...

My professors noticed something was wrong, but I couldn't tell them what it was... my sahobs, Tom, Chris and few others... I think they knew before I told them, but they couldn't help... it just wasn't a world that they lived in... honestly, I was kinda jealous of their ignorance to the inner workings of this life... it was to the point where I *damn* sure didn't want to know what I knew because the only way to know it, was by some really fucked up on the job training.

I had trouble at school because of what was going on in the streets... and I had trouble in the streets because, well, that's what happens in the streets.

I had trouble at home because Shawn is a fuckin' head case that unfortunately for me, has the best pussy and head that I've encountered up to this point, and it has seriously clouded my judgment.

So what do I do?

I start moving even more weight. I figured 'what the fuck?'... if I'm gonna be stressed out, why not be *rich* and stressed out... stupid, I know, but it made sense to me at the time, so that's what I did. I started givin' Link better prices, which means he was movin' shit even quicker than before. That meant that the fuckin' Russians were thrilled... well... except for Vlad, but that's because he was an asshole for the sake of being anasshole... the last thing he wanted was for me to be livin' up to what Vikktor always thought I'd be... a motherfuckin' coke movin' *machine*... now mind you, I wasn't no Pablo Escobar cat, but I did have visions of bein' the new and improved Peanut King or Lil Melvin, older cats that ran Bmore and played by the rules so when they came home, home was there for *them*... I'd studied how cats like them moved, how they came up, and more importantly, how they fell... and I would be *damned* if I went out like Rayful... he was a cold *beast* in this shit, but that nigga is a perfect example of what I was determined to avoid... a meteoric rise with an even more spectacular downfall caused by somethin' stupid, and turnin' into a damn rat... that was *NOT* gon' be me... not that I was movin shit like *that* nigga, but I felt like if I ever did get to that level, I was gon' make sure that I moved smarter.

A few months passed and Link had Mosher and Calhoun pumpin'... I mean, like, *dope* traffic pumpin'! You would've thought we had 'Killer Bee' or 'Homicide' bags out there, but nope... no heroin, no scramble... just some of the best ready rock in West Baltimore ... my cooking skills had improved, and that was *sayin'* somethin', 'cause I was already *that nigga* when it came to cookin'... yes, I was *still* cookin my own shit, because *no,* I ain't trust nobody else to cook my own shit... Link was movin' about a half a day between the Sandtown spot and some chick he knew out Cherry Hill. For some reason, he wanted me to meet her and it felt kinda like when Melvin wanted me to meet *him...* so this time, I didn't stall the meeting the next timehe mentioned it.

He gave her my number and we ended up meeting out Westport... I wanted to see what her area was lookin' like... how one-time was out there, what the stick-up boy potential was... basic shit I need to know before puttin' somebody on for real. We rode around in her Legend sedan scopin' Spellman Court... she said she had 2600 on lock, so I figured these goofy muhfuckahs on the wall were all with her in some capacity... they was jive raggedy, but they had numbers, so it ended up workin' out for them.

Legend Girl actually had a good thing goin' out here, but she didn't have a steady supply, which is where Link came in... sometimes the problem was she could be needy, and with Link tryin' to blow Sandtown tha fuck up, he just didn't have time to flood that block *and* Cherry Hill... there was *no* way he could keep an eye on what he needed to watch in two places at once... I saw the potential in the area and didn't feel that the annoyance level was high enough to leave that kinda money out there... plus... it never hurt to have multiple weight spots... you'd always be a tennis shoe hustler if only stayed on them corners... the goal is to *supply* the corners, not be on 'em. From there, supply the guys that supply the corners... from there, supply the guys that supply the guys that supply the corners... it was all about vertical integration... the higher up you get, the harder you are to touch, however, it also means you have the potential for a much harder fall.

I needed to continue movin' bricks to keep the Russians happy (read: keep me alive), as well as to keep shit movin' like I needed to... people were depending on me for payroll and some mo' shit, and I had to keep that goin'... plus, I was stashin' shit away from every cycle for the day when I 'retired'... I had no idea when that would be, but I knew that there was *no* way I could do this shit forever... that's what got a lot of other cats knocked... they started believing that the barber shops, the laundromats, the storefront car dealerships, and all the other bullshit that they bought to try to legitimize and wash the cash, *actually* made them 'clean' while they were still workin' out... when in reality, all it did was make them sloppy... at the end of the day, we were all *still* just drug dealers, and the Feds knew it... they were just waiting for the right time to 'remind' us of that fact.

Shit usually never goes down on a Sunday around here... corner boys tread lighter, not too much gunplay... it was kind of a 'cool-out' day from goin' hard the rest of tha week... it was some old head shit that most people generally respected... most, but clearly, not *all*.

People still sold drugs on Sunday... people still used drugs on Sunday... and some people got killed over drugs... on Sunday.

So the first thing I'm thinking when I get a call... at the house... from a blocked number is 'don't answer the phone because it's a call from a blocked number', but my dumb-ass picked up anyway.

"Carlos, Baby... did you miss me?" The voice on the other end of the line was unfamiliar, but she sounded so sexy that I wished that it *was*... not wanting to fuck up what might be a phat as shit bitch that I forgot about, I play along.

"Now, how could I forget *yo* sexy ass?" I replied.

"Ummm" she moaned ..."That's good to hear Papi... now... WHERE THE *FUCK* IS **MY MONEY?!?**"

"The fuck is this??" I said, trying to stay calm and quiet so as not to wake Shawn's ass... we were up for a good part of the night into the morning argu- fucking, and I *did not* wanna her ass up right now.

The 'argu' part of us argu-fuckin started because someone broke into her car at work, and she mystically-magically linked it back to me since I was a bail bondsman... and bail bondsmen help get criminals out of jail so they can do shit like break into her bullshit ass Subaru... and because it was Shawn, that made *perfect* sense to her... nevermind the fact that she was a fuckin' correctional officer down Baltimore City Jail and niggas that's hittin' streetside sometimes tend to take their anger out on the fuckin' CO's cars for all the fuck shit they do to inmates... some turnkeys think niggas don't have release dates and act like whole asses, and since a lot of their cars are parked directly across from where they let you out when you get released, fuckin 'em up was pretty common... soon as you come out and look slightly to the right, they're all just sittin' there.

There's supposed to be a CO that watches the lot, but that shit rarely happens... your tax dollars not at work and shit... but nope... *that* thought *never* crossed her mind.

"AGENT. MUTHAFUCKIN'. WARD. *THAT'S* WHO THE FUCK THIS IS, NIGGA."

Agent Ward? Oh shit! The Fed wit' tha phat ass! I don't think she ever said her name, but even if she did, I was so busy lookin' at her frame that I wouldn't have remembered any way...

"So, Agent Ward..."I said bein' careful to not play that officer shit seein' as how she's callin' me at home... on a Sunday... plus, I knew if

Shawn heard the word 'agent', her nosey ass would stay quiet and play sleep to listen in for somethin' to throw in my face later..."what can I do for you? I ain't know Feds worked on Sunday..."

"We work EV-UH-REE day nigga, and when it comes to you playah... *twice* on Sunday. I told you when we first met to go bake that cake... now... seein' as how that was some time ago, you should have baked *several* cakes... time to pay up."

Ok. Here's the thing...shakedowns by the cops were a normal thing in this shit... but that was by the *cops*... payin' off a muhfuckah rollin' a radio car was just a cost of doin' business ... it was just easier to pay 'em off then to have to deal wit' tha bullshit that came with not payin' 'em off... but a *Fed?* That was some new shit on me, 'cuz. Real biz, I didn't think I was *that* important enough to be catchin' this kinda attention... but fuck it, since I had it, let's see what tha bitch had to say...

"How much *Agent* Ward? How much paper is it gon' take to make you go the fuck away?"

"Well... it's not money I want now... I did at first... l mean, we've been watchin' your suppliers for a minute now, and I figured I'd hit you up for some side cash... but now that I see that you're movin' some *shit,* I'm thinkin' you could lead to bigger and better things... believe me... if I only wanted money from you, l'da tapped you out a week after I pulled you on 695... naaahhh playuh... you gon' pay me in soooo much more than money."

"Ummmm... so, what the fuck do you want?! You still ain't told me exactly what it is that you want from me!"

"Simple... I want Vikktor."

Shit. Fuck. Shitfuck.

"Who tha fuck is Vikktor?" Yeah... I know... as soon as I said that shit, I knew I'd played myself.

"Lil nigga... you know you need to stop playin yaself, for REAL... you *know* who tha fuck Vikktor is, and you *know* I know that you know who tha *fuck* Vikktor is... and I also *know* that you WILL give me Vikktor!! Shit... bringin' his ass in will make me agent of the DECADE, and if *you* don't wanna catch a linebacker number worth of Fed time, you WILL help me."

Suddenly, payin' this bitch off seemed like a bonus... a bonus that I clearly would not be able to take advantage of... and now, this bitch is trynna make me choose between a death sentence and... well... a long, *drawn out* death sentence! wasn't trynna do either, and   DAMN sure wasn't gonna work with her phat ass AT ALL... I was gonna play her over-ambitious ass like a piano but l needed some time to figure out how to pull that off... and I had to jive put up a fight so she wouldn't know that I was trynna to play her... she obviously knew what type of dude I was, and if I just went along, she'd know that I was bullshittin' ... and if I put up too much of a fight, she'd a Is o know I was bullshittin'...

"Aight bitch, check this out..."

"BITCH?!? WHO *THA FUCK* YOU THINK YOU TALKIN TO?!?! I WILL RUN YA BITCH ASS IN ON A HUMBLE AND...

"AIGHT, CHILL!! SHIT! All this screamin' and shit ain't gettin' neither one of us nowhere! Lemme get tha fuck outta bed, get through this Sunday, and let's pick this shit back up, say, Wed?"

"Nice try nigga... we'll talk Monday." Since my Sunday was obviously not gon' be spent chillin', I went ahead and got to work on this new problem.

If I went directly to Vikktor about this to warn him, I knew between Vlad's bullshit and Vikktor's natural paranoia, the decision to kill me to be on the safe side would be made pretty fuckin' quickly... if I *didn't* let them know, they'd think I had something to dowith 'em bein' set up, and that would be bad for more than *just* me... decisions, decisions... then it hit me... there *was* a way out! All I had to do was figure out a way to effectively re-arrange the pieces on the board... Ward had fucked up when she told me she wanted Vikktor... it wasn't *that* she told me, it was the *way* that she told me.

She made it *really* clear that getting' Vikktor was more important to her than any amount of money... l knew she had an idea of what kinda paper I could and do pull in, and I also knew that I wasn't the *only* pockets that she could tap, so this Vikktor shit was hella personal for her... so personal that if I played it right, I could turn that shit against her... I needed some Boat, and some creativity.

Leavin' out the house with Shawn was always kinda sketchy 'cause I never knew what was gonna set her off... when she's cool, it's a beautiful thing... really liked the fact that she needed no make up to be a beast, and her body's tha shit... could've had a bit more titty, but she more than made up for it wit' ass and a natural beauty... kinda like a model... *if* that model ate cheesesteaks and chicken boxes... she's small framed, so it amazes me how carries all that ass without bein' sloppy, but, she does... and I *very much* appreciated that.

"C'mon Babe... you look fine and it ain't like we showin' off tonight *anyway.*" She was all in the mirror like she really needed it, when she really didn't. I think all those years of her parents arguin', her father bein' a dick, and any other number of things (bein' around all girls at Western, dealin' with wack niggas, etc.) just made her feel bad about herself... she was like a lot of chicks I knew and knew of... *maaadd* pretty, but saw nothin' but ugly when they looked in themirror... so they fucked, sucked, and did what they thought would make 'em attractive, only to end up playin' themselves in the process.

"Well if we *not* showin' off, let's take *my* car." She had me there... whatn't *no way* we were takin that borin' ass Subaru to D. C. when I had tha Caddy on stand- by... shit, I'd rather take the Mustang, and that's *damn* near a full race car, instead of the Subaru... shit was like a sleeping pill on wheels... plus, there wasn't enough Morning Fresh in the world to get rid of that weird smell it always had from her daughter throwin' up in the car... l know she was young, but that 'lil girl had some serious stomach issues.

"I guess we *are* showin' off then Babe!" I laughed and enjoyed the moment, knowing that it was really the start of the countdown to another argument.

The trip to D. C. was gon' serve a few purposes ... Shawn would always get antsy when I left out at night, and since I wasn't gon' take her on any 'bail bondsman' business, this would be a good chance for us to just be out. There was also the fact that the only place you gon' get *real* mumbo sauce is in the City... like go-go PA tapes, DDTP gear, and good temple tapers, it was a D. C. thang... mumbo sauce made *errrythang* taste better, so whenever I was in the City, I made sure to stop at a Danny's and get some wings, fried rice, and a rack of mumbo sauce... youd'a thought I was smugglin' coke the way I'd pack that shit in the car!

Then there was the *real* reason why we needed to come to D. C. *tonight... I* knew I could get that Boat that'd have you runnin' down tha street and geekin' out ya clothes... yea... dat *butt nekkid* shit that'll fuck ya *right* up... and it just so *happened* that a dude at Danny's was sellin' some... I know... what a coincidence, right?

I hadn't figured out exactly how yet, but the loose plan was to Agent Booth to ingest the shit somehow ... coffee... doughnut. .. shit, I ain't know, but I knew if I could get it in her system, I'd have her ass dead to rights... that shit comes to rest in ya spinal fluid, so it ain't like you can just wait 30 days or drink some cleanse shit to test clean... her knowin' that alone *should* be enough to put her ass in check... at least I was hoping so.

Shawn and I got home, ate dinner ... fucked the shit outta each other, then went to sleep... all in all, it wasn't a bad evening.

Helloooo, Monday. I called Agent Ward to get this shit over with... I still didn't know how I was gonna pull this off, but I *did* know that waitin' around wasn't gon' help matters much. She wanted me to meet her near the Woodlawn police building...it wasn't an actual DEA facility, but the shit was close enough since them muahfuckahs worked with each other anyway. I figured she wanted to be close to 'her people' without actually bringing me too close to her people...the police and DEA are all cops, but they have their own individual way of doing things...she wanted to be able to have a rack of law enforcement around in case I started some shit, but she didn't want them to be DEA because then she'd run the risk of having to explain what just happened if things went really sideways...basically, she could lie to the police more effectively than she could to her own people.

I was cutting through Lord Baltimore Drive and got a call from Agent Ward... apparently, something on her end came up and this wasn't gonna happen today after all... that shit was cool wit' me, 'cause fa real, I had *no* idea how I was gon' get the wet into her system... I hung up the phone, threw tha wet in tha street and hoped a truck or somethin' would run it over.

Now that Ward was off my ass for the time bein', I focused on getting' back to that grind... I had money to stand on and tha shit wasn't gon' get itself. Since I was still close to the apartment, I figured I'd go further away from it... I'd left on a good note and I didn't see any sense in goin' back and fuckin' it up... I'd see Shawn later on... or not.

I had an 11:15 class that I knew I was gonna be late for, but I also knew that Prof. Bullock wasn't gon' be there anyway, so it really didn't matter. I had the syllabus, so I really only showed up when I had something to turn in or for the occasional critique session... but all that was bullshit... l was really coming to class because it gave me an escape from what I was doing and why I was doing it... it was weird... l was great at being two different people that in their own respective worlds, couldn't *stand* each other... imagine living with that kinda turmoil in ya head every day.

See, I would check out all these people on campus... men, women... all of 'em, and would think, 'why are you *really* here?' It was a well-known fact that Howard University was tha shit as far as Black colleges and universities went, it was called 'Mecca' for a very good reason... yeah, Hampton, Clark-Atlanta, Morgan and the like all talked shit about being the best, but everybody knew that when it comes down to it, you either *went* to Howard, or you *wanted* to go to Howard and just ended up settling for some other place... don't get mad at me, I don't make the rules.

I wasn't proud of what I was doing *off* campus, but I was proud to be able to be *on* campus... college is a privilege and bein' at Howard was some fairytale shit for me... so like I said, I would wonder why some of the 'beautiful people' were wasting the experience ... these mu'hfuckahs really bought into that 'Different World' shit likereal life was a Cosby Show spinoff.

That shit intrigued me and pissed me off at the same time... it intrigued me that there *were* apparently a *rack* of Black folks that *really* had it like that to be able to raise their kids in a way that had them thinkin' that there wasn't shit that *they couldn't* have...'cause for the most part, it whatn't shit that they *didn't* have... and it pissed me off 'cause a gang of 'em didn't appreciate just how good they hadit.

I'd hear 'em talking... bitchin' about what Gucci sneakers they were gon' hit they folks up for... or what car they were gon' hit they folks up for... or what bag they was gon' hit they folks up for, or... well... you get the idea... shit, I was hustling, so I was *supposed* to have 'more than the average bear'... I was takin' penitentiary chances pretty much every day and havin' dough was the byproduct of doing *that*... but these kids had it like that just by callin their parents... then I realized that at the end of the day, it was simply jealousy on my part. I *wanted* to 'have it like that' *without* getting it how I did. Again... l was no Nino Brown, Tony Montana level type cat, but I'll be *damned* if this shit ain't stressin' me tha fuck out, so I *really* appreciated the dough I was gettin'... but like I said, I whatn't proud of how I was gettin' it, and at times (mostly when I was on campus), the embarrassment of what I was doing really hit me. Hard.

I turned in my project, hung out on The Yard for a few, then went to Sarah's for a jumbo bacon cheeseburger combo... after that, I got back in the car, and headed home to sell more drugs.

Real biz... this shit was gettin' old, but the money... *Cuz*... the *money*... that shit was more addictive than the shit we were sellin'. We spent a lotta time talkin' 'bout *'dem fiends this and 'dem fiends that'* when we were just as bad *if not worse*... shit... the fiends *at least* had an excuse by havin' tha disease of an addiction based on a chemical dependence ... only excuse us hustlers had was that we was greedy as *fuck* and wanted *more* dough than the nigga sittin' next to us and ain't care how we got it... so who was *really* more fucked up?

The next day, I was in The Vault makin' my rounds, all the while wonderin' when Agent Ward was gonna pop back up... l hadn'theard back from her (not that I was looking to), and that concerned me... she was on a mission *for real* and I needed to be aware of what she was up to... attention from a Fed is bad enough, but a Fed with a personal beef? That shit is just treacherous.

I'd decided to take Link's advice and put Legend Girl on... havin' a spot out Cherry Hill was intriguing to me 'cause the area *definitely* gets money as long as you're from there... them Cherry Hill boys are real serious about protecting their shit, and many a nigga found that

DUMMY.

out the hard way that trynna set up shop without goin through the 'proper channels' just ain't gon' work out there... plus, if you already out Cherry Hill, getting' somethin' goin' out Westport was jive simple if you played it right... niggas *got rich* fuckin' around out there, and I wanted a piece... you know... for my retirement fund.

Anyway, I dropped off the package to Legend Girl... it was small, only 56g... l figured if she fucked it up, it was only 2 O's, but if she didn't, well, we'd see how it goes. Two ounces was enough to tempt a nigga to run off and if that happened, it's a small price to pay to find out the type of people you were workin' with... besides, if that *did* happen, I was already good to go as far as collectin' the debt... l knew where all of 'em laid their heads, and more importantly, *they* knew I knew and that the tools weren't for show... if they came out, the flame show was next... 230 grain . 45 rounds get it IN... it was that simple. I wasn't no 'supa-thug-nigga-killa' type cat, but lalso learned early on that you couldn't just *talk* about certain shit, you had to actually *do* certain shit, and while some of it was pretty fucked up, it was necessary if you wanted to continue in this line of work.

It was also another reason that this shit was stressin' me out, and why I found myself thinking of a *way out*...even if you don't have to put in work on the regular, the fact that you have to be ready to do it *all* the time just wears on you...maybe not for everybody but *damn* sure for me.

When I left Legend Girl, she told me to watch my beeper 'cause she was gon' be callin soon... l said OK thinkin' it would be tomorrow sometime before I heard back. It wasn't like I thought she was a scrub or nothin', I just didn't have any point of reference for how long she'd take since this was the first package. Plus, with the extra I was chargin' for the consignment factor, she was actually payin more than what it was worth, but that was all part of the test.

About 3 hrs. later, she paged me to let me know that she was finished, and 30 seconds after that, I knew I had a new business partner. Link was right... Legend Girl... she was a *beast*.

I'd charged her $2400 for that work, and yeah, I knew that what was waaay too much for 56 grams, but like I said, it was the first one and it was a test... a test she passed with flying colors... those two ounces were actually extra off the cook-up, so it was all profit for me... so, in effect, I'd just made $800 an hour.

Moments like this made it very hard to walk away... no matter how much of a headache the other parts of 'the job' were, wasn't a lot of other shit I could do and make $800 an hour... well... not a lot of other *legal* shit anyway.

Wasn't long before Legend Girl was movin' quarters for me... once muhfuckahs found out that good Westside ready was available in South Baltimore, sheeeeiiitt, it was *on!* She was movin' 250 grams in a day, day and a half... she coulda' moved more if I gave it to her, but she was still on some consignment shit so a quarter key was my limit... and it would be both a good and bad thing in the long run.

Link was movin' shit like a muhfuckah too, but that wasn't no surprise... I was hittin' him of with half a brick like every 2-3 days... and he was *payin'* for his shit. He'd told me early on that he wasn't tryin' to be fronted no longer than he needed to be, and he was *not* bullshit- tin'. Niggas thought I was crazy for lettin' bricks of ready ready go for $22,000 a half, but to tell the truth, I ain't give a shit... by the time I was done with my cooks, I was making at least $5000 in extras off each half, and for Link, I gave it to him for $16Gs flat... his money was always steady, was always right, and he never came wit' no excuses... l know for a fact that more than a few times that he wasn't *really* ready 'cause he still had shit out on the street, but he went into his own stash to keep that consistency with me... I respected the shit outta him for that. It was a simple thing that you'd think would be the norm, but it wasn't... his business game is only slightly overshadowed by his violence game which made him the perfect candidate to become my right hand man... l was gon' do a bit more, set him up with the Russians, and fade out...

I'd still be getting some money from the streets but wouldn't be in 'em at all anymore... only thing I'd be touchin' would be money... just a college student installing stereo systems until I got a 'real' gig... yeah... just a few more moves and Link would be 'the man' with me in the background getting paid for puttin' him there.

Link had been fuckin' wit' me about comin' down the way more... l wasn't tellin' him that most of the time it was 'cause I was either doin' somethin' for school or the stereo shop, and that the other times, I just ain't wanna hang out down there... it was hot as *fuck* down tha way and 'new regular faces' only made it hotter. The knockers ain't even try to sneak up on some jump-out shit anymore... they would just sit across the street, take pictures, then stroll across and start fuckin' witcha... if you showed up in more than 3-4 pictures, you was on tap to get fucked wit and fucked up... but Link... man, Link *lives* for that shit!

This nigga shoots at Foxtrot 'just because', so he really ain't pressed about muhfuckahs takin' pictures...he's like 'Nigga, I grew up here and came up here... y'all bitches just punchin' a fuckin' clock...so when y'all muhfuckahs punch out and go home, I'm *already* home, so what tha fuck I look like *runnin'*??

While Link makes some damn good points, I had *enough* trouble in my life to *make more* by getting' put in somebody's file by way of a picture, or shootin' at Baltimore City's helicopters 'just because'. I'd go down there, sit onthe stoop for a minute, maybe eat a chicken box over some business talk, and then I was *out*... Link's the supastar down there and that was fine by me... the *less* you're known, the *fewer* that can describe you if shit goes down.

Which was why I was only slightly surprised when I got the call from one his homeboys sayin' he was locked up... l figured it was because of some 'block shit', and I was right, it just wasn't the block shit I thought it was.

Seems that Link fucked the wrong bitch which by itself would've been fine, but this one was only 15, so when Link was on some 'fuck and get up' type shit, shorty thought otherwise... she just knew that Link was now 'her man', and when he let her know she wasn't, she called 'rape'... *and* the police.

Link fucked the girl on a Thursday and was locked up that Saturday... clearly, Baltimore City takes that type shit *seriously.*

Link's man was calling to get some bail money together but I didn't have it... well, I did, but not really... I'd just bought a bunch of stuff for the apartment, paid Shawn's credit cards off, and some more shit, so while I had it, I really didn't... Link's my man, but I wasn't touchin' my retirement money for nobody... besides, his man had already said that his Aunt was gon' put her house up, so I wasn't too worried.

Of course, when he got out, Link was bitchin' about how 'niggas move all this coke and couldn't come up with his bail'... I just told him he'd gotten locked up at a bad time for me, and that $20K to the bail-bondsman was gon' be a problem right then... plus, I still had to stay off of everyone's radar so I could avoid Agent Ward *and* stay in play to make moves with the Russians... he was cool wit' that... l think he was expectin' some crazy-ass story, but the truth made perfect sense.

Besides... he knew I would look out for him on the next package... what can I say... my coke was tha shit and *his pockets* knew it... gettin' a nigga paid said 'my fault slim' better than *actually* sayin' 'my fault slim'.

Link was out by the end of that week and about 30 seconds after he touched down, I had him hooked up... l hit him off with the regular package *plus* another half on me... needless to say, he was *very* okay with that.

I left Link to do what he does and headed over to check on Legend Girl. The last few packages were movin' well and I was considerin' bumpin' her up to even more... shit, she was doin' so well I was thinkin' about puttin' some BB's on that Legend she drove... it was an ego thing for me... since I wasn't gon' be drivin' that type shit, I could live vicariously through the niggas I had workin' for me... that way, niggas would know that those who I fucked wit was gettin money... when word on the street is that you can not only eat, you can *eat well* with a nigga, that shit is its own recruitin' speech... unfortunately, it also attracts niggas that just wanna eat but don't wanna put that work in, *other* than murkin' tha nigga that's feedin' everybody else. I wasn't worried about that too too much for tha time being 'cause tha niggas I was feedin' wanted to *keep* gettin' fed... as such, these cats would knock a nigga off *wit' tha quickness* to keep me in play... but I also wasn't stupid enough to think that that was enough to always protect me... after all, it was like that convo between Frank and Tony in 'Scarface', never underestimate the *other* guy's greed.

"So what's up Tee? You trynna 'move on up' like a Jefferson? Legend Girl looked surprised ... I never really called her by name, and I still hadn't... but even me calling her by the first letter of her name made her know I was comin' wit' some shit... some *good* shit that she needed to not only listen to, but to actually *hear*... I was about to take a chance on both of us... her with the increased weight I was about to give her, and me with... well... the potential for increased *wait* because of it.

"Ya shit is on-point..."

No need for the formalities of using the first letters of names anymore.

"You movin' shit real good... no problems wit' my money comin' back... no askin' for more time after you already said when you gon' be done... l like that shit... how you feel about movin some more weight?"

"Sheeeiit, yo! Hell *muthaphuckin' yeah* I wanna move some more!! Hmmphh... well, *she* seemed excited.

"Cool, cool... now look... you already know what I was chargin' you before, but since I'm 'bout ta step you up, I'ma give you a 'lil break on the price... the more you move and the quicker you move it, the more I can try to hook you up... and when you ready, you start buyin' direct from me... I'll hook you up even more for that cash and carry, ya feel me?"

"Damn 'Los! Link always did say you was cool denna' fan! How much more you talkin' bout?"

"Enough to cause both you and me to have real problems if ya ass don't carry it right. I'ma hit you off with this QB and see how quick you move this shit.

She was real cool wit that shit... l mean, who wouldn't be? Nine O's was a lotta shit to front a muhfuckah, but I knew where she laid her head, where her man worked, where her cousins stayed, what all

DUMMY.

they asses drove... and she *knew* that I knew it... if it came down to it, business is business, and *business* would be handled if need be... I hit her off and rolled out.

Melvin gettin' killed was still fuckin' wit me. I kept wonderin' what I could've done differently to change the course of that day... l mean... even if it was by just a few minutes, it could've been enough to save 'em... or at least push that shit off to a time when we were together and I could've had has back... I dunno... like I said... the shit was *fuckin'* with me.

I kept feelin' like I was the reason he was dead, and what was even more fucked up was the fact that I was questioning why it wasn't me... l mean for real... l had done *way* more fucked up shit than he did and probably had it comin'... so why him and not me? I mean, seriously, even though Melvin knew a rack of muhfuckahs that *could* kill him, none of them would... he was *Melvin*, and everybody knew it, so him gettin killed 'on his own' just didn't make sense...but the thought of somebody possibly killing him to get my attention?

That shit was making more and more sense every day, but I just couldn't figure out *who* it was that would do that .

These feelings would come and go, but the fact that they existed at all was a problem... with what I was dealing with, I just couldn't afford to keep havin' shit like this 'pop up' in my mind.

Oh goody... Shawn's calling.

Since the day was already winding down and I had no other stops to make, I figured I'd try to have a nice evening with her... it really did bother me that when we were good, we were great, but when we weren't, it was the fuckin' worst... l really wanted to have this be a 'good' evening. We got somethin' to eat and it actually went well... I didn't even trip when the waiter tried to hollah at her on the sly... I understood... she's attractive and was phat as shit, what dude *wouldn't* wanna fuck her? I paid the bill, tipped him $50 bucks, thanked him for the service, and reminded him as we left that while he's jackin' off to her tonight, I'll actually *be* fuckin her... *well.*

The fact that I said this with a hand full of her ass while she was looking straight at him really seemed to drive my point home. What can I say? I'm a hopeless romantic.

Things were actually goin' pretty good... Legend Girl was movin shit so fast it was almost annoying... 5-6 hrs. after I would hit her off, she was pagin' me to tell me she was done... but like I said, it was *almost* an annoyance ... I wasn't *'bout* to bitch about my money comin' back

DUMMY.

wit tha quickness. Link's lawyer was postponin' the rape case seemingly indefinitely ... they were goin' for the 'lets-delay-this-a-million-times and-hope-that-she-doesn't-show-up on-the-one-day-that-we-do' defense... it worked well in Bmore, so, I get it.

Vikktor was happy with the money I was bringin' in, which pissed Vlad off even more (always a good thing)... I was gettin' projects for school done and showin' up for classes on a regular basis...well, regular *for me* anyway, and even more surprising was the fact that Shawn and I were really gettin' along well... l mean, we still argued here and there, but it wasn't as bad as it had been, which was *very* cool.

One of Link's boys hit me up, which was strange since the last time that happened, Link was gettin' knocked for that 'rape' charge. It had been a while since that happened, and since I knew Link's lawyer was real close to gettin' the whole thing tossed out, I was wonderin' what he'd gotten himself into *this* time. I'd just seen him earlier that day, so it was odd that his man was callin' and not him.

'Whassup, Ant, y'all good? Where my man at?' I asked, wanting to speak directly with Link so I could find out what was goin' on.

'Link gone yo... he *gone.*'

'Da fuck you mean he gone?' I asked jokingly, still not putting two and two together..."Where'd he go? I know this nigga ain't go off wit' anotha one of them young bitches down tha way... this nigga ain't learned shit, huh?' I said figuring that Link was off in some young pussy, about to start all over with this rape case shit.

'Naww, yo... Los... Link dead. We was at the pool hall... niggas was beefin with us, we fucked they asses up and went back to playin' pool... then them niggas came back *blastin'*... laid Link out as we was comin' out the door... I got hit too, but I ran to get the shit off the tire to blast back, but they was gon' by the time I ran back'.

'Hold tha fuck up, Ant!! HOLD UP! You left that nigga there by *himself*??? 'Los, it wasn't no helpin' him, fa real! They hit him wit a '57 nigga, from like five feet away!! One of them shits went *through him and hit me!* Shit, he was dead before he hit the ground 'Los!'

See, this was the shit I was tryin' to warn Link about... niggas get real funny style when you start fuckin' wit they paper... and this shit had 'fuck y'all niggas, we'll just kill you and take over' written all over it... everybody knew Link and how he got down... and they also knew it wasn't gon' be a whole lotta talkin' when it came down to whose toes was getting' stepped on or whose pockets was getting' lighter... Link was a real killer, and niggas *knew* it... they also knew that the only way to effectively deal with a killer is to kill 'em first... that's why the niggas that got Link wasn't really worried 'bout Ant and them when they were blastin... they weren't just gunnin' for Link, they were gunnin' for his area too and they knew that without Link, they'd lack that focused direction... they'd still be dangerous, but moreso to themselves than to others because they were gon' be busy on some revenge shit.

The niggas that killed 'em was just gon' profit off the confusion and fill the void they damned selves...fiends don't like a whole lotta conflict when they trynna cop, so while it's beef and other rah-rah shit goin' on up the street, down the street, niggas is gettin' money... it was a diversionary tactic that has worked since forever and will continue to do so because it's so effective, so I *knew* what was coming next. 'Ant, listen to me... get off tha block. Get dem otha niggas off the block... homicide 'gon be down there wit tha quickness, and...' 'Sheeiiitt, *dem niggas already* here!' 'Ant... *get off tha block* and take *errybody* with you... lemme know who's talkin to homicide when we meet at the spot.'

I was pissed that I had to remind Ant to get tha fuck off the block... that shit was just common sense, *especially* since tha nigga was leakin'... shit, they coulda held him on *that shit* alone, and *would* have had they seen his dumb ass... I needed to know how much of what I'd hit Link off with was out, what was ready to go out, and more importantly, where it was.

I hadn't even stopped to process tha fact that Link was gone... the last conversation I had with him was gon' be the last I ever *would have* with him, and that was startin' to sink in.

Ant hit me back with the news that I thought he would... and long story short, I was gon' have to take a loss.

According to him, Link had hit off enough people for it to be hard as fuck to get that shit back, especially now that everybody had heard Link got murked... all it was gon' be was a bunch of niggas lyin' sayin they hadn't got shit yet from Link. I knew it wasn't true, but the only way to enforce that shit would've been to beat the shit outta everyone that got hit off and or start shootin niggas... yeah, my point woulda been made, but niggas had started to get that 'itch to snitch'.

Link could keep these niggas in line because he came up with them... l was just a mystery man that they were gon' be forced to try their hand with... can't say that I would blame them, but when my response of snatchin' their 'lil bad-ass kids from that unlicensed daycare up the street, or getting a bitch to repeadtedly punch they Mama in the mouth, *that* was the kinda attention that they weren't used to and *then* they wanted to become upstanding citizens and get one-time involved. I didn't need that kinda heat on top of Link getting got... and since Ant wasn't exactly in a position to fill in for Link, I had to figure out how to keep this shit flowin' *without* losin' the 'behind the scenes' strength I'd built... a king can fall, but a kingmaker can *always* make another king.

I told Ant to get what he could from what was out there... sheisty ass nigga was gon' come up, but that was cool... niggas like him burned through money like shit through a goose so I knew he'd be back soon enough. Meanwhile, I had to re-focus on my Spelman Court connection ... Legend Girl was flowin and even though Link was gone, she was a soldier ... she evenhad her cousin and nephew in the mix. Her cousin was cute, but on the shy side... her nephew... well... he was a possession charge just lookin' for some place to happen, but he wasn't *my* problem, so I didn't give a *fuck*... my money was comin' back and it gave me one less thing to have to worry about... right until it *didn't*.

"Ay 'Los, I gotta problem." Seeing as Legend Girl *never* had any problems, I thought she was 'gon hit me with a 'we got robbed and I can't pay you' story... I was not in the mood for *that* bullshit... even though I'd made so much extra off her ass in the past that she coulda fucked off a whole brick and it wouldn't have phased me, the price *was* what the price *was*.

As it turns out, I would quickly learn that a claim of robbery would have actually been slightly easier to deal with.

"What's the problem? No, better yet, meet at the spot... gimme a few." She knew that 'gimme a few' meant 'right now'... whatever shit she was 'bout to drop on me, I wanted to look in her eyes as she said it. I pulled up to the spot and saw the Legend was pulling up at the same time. I hopped out and let her see that I was motioning for her to get out the car and join me for a walk... if she had somebody with her, they were gon' have to hop out or drive along... either way, I would know they were there and where they were. She joined me with no prob, and we started walking...then she started talking.

"'Los, you still got them thangs?"

"You called me out here to ask me about some *bricks*?!?" I was pissed 'cause I was like, you *know* I do, so why you wastin my time askin'? "Noooo, nooo, not coke... them *thang* thangs... blickies...*tools*, niggah! I need some *shit*...it's some young boys from a couple courts over tryin to take the Wall, and I wanna clap 'em out.

The Wall was one of the most money gettin' spots *in* Cherry Hill... Spelman Court as a whole was steady clockin', but The Wall was like the flagship spot...if you had The Wall and could hold it down, you basically had Spelman Court on lock.

"Yeah, I got some shit, but tha fuck I look like givin' em to you? If I gotta supply you *and* arm you, tha *fuck* am I fuckin witchu you for?

I might as well get some niggas of my own down there, have them lay it down, and just take tha shit over for all dat!"

"'Los, you know *mutha-fuckin'* well you ain't gon' bring no new niggas down there and they live to tell about it... we may beef with ourselves, but let a new nigga come through... we *quick* to put our shit to the side to cook a new nigga and you *know* that!"

She was right... like I said, that whole Cherry Hill/ Westport area *did* not take kindly to newcomers, and like she said, they'll stop beefin' with each other and join forces long enough to get rid of *anything or anyone* that they perceived as an outside threat... you gotta respect that kinda shit... I didn't *like* it *at all,* but I did respect it... besides... it wasn't like I had a choice.

"Look, I ain't bringin' no fuckin' armory down this bitch! Last thing I need is you muhfuckahs puttin' more bodies on my shit, then fuckin' round and tossin' my shit... them shits cost money!!"

See, I didn't really have a problem with the guns bein' used, I mean, that's why I bought 'em... my thing was that I paid good money for 'em because they were clean when I got 'em, and they had never been confiscated ... they were bought under fake names in states that didn't require a shell casing (gotta love the deep South and Midwest), so once I brought 'em back here, there was no record of them existing here... they weren't in my name, and there was no shell casing, so I could let off a hundred rounds (and sometimes did), and there was nothing for one time to reference the casings or rounds to... like I said, to Maryland, the guns just didn't exist.

Then I had an idea that could solve both of our problems. "Gimme $800, and I'll get you a shotgun. That way, ain't no forensics 'cause it's pellets."

"Damn 'Los, I could go buy one for that!"

"Good, then go buy tha muthaphucka then... I don't want tha fuckin' hassle any damn way!"

"No, no... ok 'Los... here. When you comin' back? 'Cause we tryin' to do this shit tonight!"

"I'll be back to drop it off in a couple hours, maybe sooner ... I'mma run back down my way, then swing back through to drop it off."

"You ain't gon' blast wit us? These niggas is trynna hit yo pockets too if think about it."

"Naaah. I ain't blastin at shit... like I said... if I gotta do all that, then why am I fuckin witchu?"

"Aight 'Los... aight... I'll see ya later."

This wasn't something that I wanted to have to do, but she had a point... these niggas that were comin after them on The Wall, were also comin after *my* money by default... I swear, there's enough junkies out here for everybody, so why muhfuckahs insisted on this 'wild cowboy takin over spots' shit is beyond me.

It wasn't like they weren't makin' money where *they* were, they just wanted more and figured The Wall was there for the taking... it's something that you kinda have to expect if you get a spot that's pumpin'... as soon as it gets known that it's makin' some dough, *that's* when the niggas that's either too lazy to build they own shit come out, or the ones that are so greedy that theirs ain't enough and they want yours too... either way, there's a specific response that has to be given, but *that* shit makes a pumpin' spot hot as fuck for all the wrong reasons... can't move *shit* while homicide is investigatin' ,and *everything* stops until they leave... bad part about *that* is, sometimes they don't leave until the spot is dead or so weak that it ain't even worth fuckin' wit until they cool all the way down, but during that time, a gang of money is just going to the next shop.

This happens a *lot* more than one might think... it's one of the reasons why spots pop up seemingly out of nowhere. 'Traditional' strips... Edmondson & Pulaski, Gold St., North & Dukeland ... they been Westside spots that as far as anybody could remember.

Of course, Eastside got spots too, but I don't fuck around like that over there, so I really couldn't say what's 'traditional' and what's not, but the Belair Edison area, Greenmount, and Waverly... they were areas that even from West you knew they been gettin money for a minute.

The little alleys and cuts that nobody gave a fuck about before, get turned into a spot when the traditional ones get too hot... somebody gets killed or anything else happens that has Five-O down the way for more than a couple days, and those alleys and cuts start to become 'transitional traditionals'. The fiends will find that good shit, so getting the customer base to be 'loyal' ain't really an issue, but sometimes settin' up shop in a different place can cause problems... for every transitional traditional, there's some other muhfuckahs that feel like you takin fries out they chicken box, and they usually gon' have somethin to say about it.

This is why I wasn't joinin' Legend Girl in her blast party... I knew the aftermath was gon' be enough of a hassle with the heat that was comin'... that area had plenty of money to get, but like I said, it wasn't easy for outsiders, so it just made sense to let them handle that shit internally... when it comes to that, shit is 'family business' and I ain't blood.

DUMMY.

I was on the way to one of my gun stashes when Shawn called. I swear she had a sick ass talent for wantin' to talk when I had some serious shit to take care of... seriously, I could have a couple hours where I'm not doin' shit, and I wouldn't hear from her... as soon as I have to handle somethin', she gotta holla at me.

"Ayy Babe? Wussupwitcha?" I led with a pleasant greeting, even though I was pretty sure she was about to bitch about something.

"Nothin' much... just missed you and wanted to hear ya voice... you busy today? You gon' be home late?"

Her being nice kinda threw me... I shouldn't be so hard on her, but damn, it wasn't like she hadn't given me enough reason to be 'cautious'. "Awww, that's cool... you miss ya man and want him to come home, huh?"

"Yeah, Baby... you know I worry about you... I see all these dudes comin' in here and yeah, some of 'em should be here... but the ones that I know just been fucked over and are here on a humble."

"Are you goin' somewhere with this depressin' ass shit?"

"YES, SMARTASS ... IF YOU WOULD LET ME FINISH...I was *saying* that *some* of the ones in here on a humble have family that are gon' be wondering where they are...then when they find out, that's gon' be even worse...I just...*Baby,* I just want to know to know that you're *always* coming home."

"I'm cool, Babe... why you buggin'?"

"Because I'm not stupid... you say you out doin bailbondsman shit, and I can't *prove* that you don't... but you and I both know that you aren't, and if you actually are, that ain't the *only* shit that you're doin'... I was ok with not knowin' in the beginning because, well, that shit was a turn-on... it kinda *still* is... but I want something *more* for us... dammit, I want more for *you*... you don't give yourself enough credit Carlos, but I see it... you could be just as successful doing other shit than the *other shit* that you do."

I ain't know where all of this was really comin' from, but it definitely wasn't no shit I was tryin to hear... not right now anyway... l had too much on my mind at the moment... l mean, she was sayin' some shit that I knew was true, but I just couldn't afford to admit right now.

"Babe, I'm *good*... I'm *cool* for real... I won't be out late... let's talk about this more when I get in, cool?""Cool Baby, I love you', but in more ways than one, I was already gone.

The Mossberg Persuader is a *really* well named shotgun ... this bitch will 'persuade' you to do damn near anything to avoid bein' shot by it... it's not quite a tactical shotgun, but it's still effective...the shotgun

DUMMY.

that's in the police car, that's a Mossberg 500... main difference between that one and this one is that I got the pistol grip on mine...can be hard on the wrist if you're not careful, but you can also conceal it better... plus, I haven't had a situation yet where I needed more than 3 shots, much less the 8 that it holds.

Plus, I used slugshot shells re- packed with rock salt... this not only helped distort the shell as it went in, it's *rock salt* being pushed into a body by a slug... l hadn't seen anyone get up from the combo since I started using it, so I stuck with it... I used to use buckshot, but that shit don't stop a nigga like a slug does.

Also... it's a *shotgun*... it's not exactly quiet and at the end of the day, if you need *more* than 3 shots for the shit that I use it for, you just shouldn't be using it at all.

I put 5 more slugshot shells in, hid it in The Vault and headed back to Legend Girl.

Wasn't no way I was gon' 'hand' her a shotgun, knowing that there was a good chance that shit might get tossed... my prints were nowhere on it, but still, that shit cost money, and why waste a perfectly good shotgun? I figured she would tell me that she 'had' to toss it, which was why I charged her $800 dollars for a $200 shotgun. Anyway, I stashed the shottie in a location near our meeting spot that I could see, but she couldn't see me. I let her know where to look, watched as she picked it up, then honked the horn when she did... she couldn't say she never got it 'cause she instinctively looked toward where the horn honk was coming from and saw me *seeing* her.

I headed back home to finish the conversation with Shawn... it's funny, but l was actually kinda looking forward to it... when she wasn't being her normal insane self, Shawn was someone I could see being with for a while... it was just sad that those times were few and far between, but fuck it, I was gonna enjoy it while it lasted, because it never lasted long.

I decided that we should go out to eat, so I suggested we go to Phillip's...she really likes seafood, and since there was no Legal Seafood close, Phillip's was cool...plus, I knew they had other stuff that they did well besides just seafood, which around here, always involved crab and other shellfish...I can't eat shellfish, so seafood spots that don't have steak or a good selection of fish are a waste of time and money for me. I found out the hard way that I was allergic shortly after Ma and I moved here. Back home in Cleveland, she would make these bangin' ass salmon croquets...I couldn't get enough of 'em! So when I saw crabcakes, I was like 'bet'; they looked like the salmon joints and since crabmeat was supposed to be better than salmon, I thought, 'cool, I'mma knock these out with tha quickness!'

DUMMY.

I got through half of one and shit started to go bad, *fast*. . . had trouble breathing and my mouth felt numb... then my stomach started hurtin' like a *bitch!* I had no idea what was going on at the time, but the trouble breathing was my throat closing in on itself, and the numbness and nausea was my body negatively reacting to proteins in the crabmeat ... a lot of times, people will say it's the iodine that does it, but trust me, I've researched it... it's the proteins... it's why if you're allergic to it, you can't even really be around it when it's being cooked... that shit goes airborne when heated and you can actually inhale it, which to your body, is the same as ingesting it... take too much of it in, and it can send you into shock and kill you... may sound like some nerd shit, but when food almost fuckin' kills you, you tend to research that shit.

Damned shame too, 'cause I really like the smell of Old Bay cooking... but since this is Baltimore, that usually means it's on crabs that I can't eat... so I make up for it by eating the shit out Utz and Herr's Old Bay potato chips... mostly UTZ, but Herr's is a damn close second.

Anyway, she ordered her usual crabcake platter, and I ordered a steak; medium rare so they have to give you a better cut of meat... we ate and had a really good conversation ... any dude with eyes would have been attracted to Shawn, but I found I was most into her when we would converse... that shit was a turn on for me because it was rare for bangin' ass women to have a tight convo game... most of 'em depended on their looks and phat asses to get 'em through life and never worked on developing themselves for anything else but fuckin' and suckin' ... shit gets old real quick, but it works on most dudes 'cause that's all they want *anyway...* I understood where they were comin' from, but that didn't make it 'right' as far as I was concerned, but with all that I had goin' on, who was I to question anybody *else's* shit?

Tha fuck can I call somebody on their shit when I'm doin' what *I'm* doin? I ain't exactly the best moral compass... I sell drugs... a *lot* of fuckin' drugs, to anybody with the money, and I don't give a fuck who ends up with them... no, I don't *want* kids or pregnant bitches gettin high off my shit, but I'd served pregnant bitches when I was goin' hand to hand because they were gonna get it from *somebody* and I wanted tha dough... I don't sell weight with a warning sticker and I don't profess to be a saint either.

Like I said ... I sell drugs ... and I'm really *fuckin'* good at it... but for as good at it as I am, I don't want to do this shit anymore... it's a job that has no sick days, the vacations are state or Federally sponsored and way too fuckin' long, and the retirement plan is usually a cold metal slab with the only upside being the fact that you're dead, so the cold doesn't matter because, well, the being dead part.

Shawn and I talked while we waited for our food to arrive... like I said, her convo game was on point, and now we were talking about our 'future'... Shawn was a handful, but at her best, she was... well... at her *best,* she had me thinking we could 'end up' with each other... but I knew that my current line of work would never allow that shit to be.

On paper, I should be able to walk away from this drug shit and be tha dude that she thinks I could be... that dude that part of her believes I am, and part of me *wants* to be as well... but at the end of the day, I can't have fuckin' feelings like that... shit'll get me fucked up or killed... but still... the shit she was talkin'... movin' away, startin' fresh somewhere sounded good to me... I'm at tha point where walkin' away sounds less and less crazy every time it's brought up.

Our food came and as we started eating, I received a call from a number that I didn't immediately recognize, so I initially ignored it... then one of the waiters came by, handed me a satellite phone, looked me straight in the eye and said, 'You *need* to take this', and then, *everyone* in the restaurant calmly got up and left... I put the phone to my head and heard...

"Carlos... this is Vikktor..."